ReSHONDA TATE BILLINGSLEY

*Her bestselling novels of family
and faith have been hailed as . . .*

"Emotionally charged . . . not easily forgotten."

—*Romantic Times*

"Steamy, sassy, sexy."

—*Ebony*

"Compelling, heartfelt."

—*Booklist*

"Full of palpable joy, grief, and soulful characters."

—*Jacksonville Free Press*

"Poignant and captivating, humorous and heart-wrenching."

—*The Mississippi Link*

Don't miss these wonderful novels!

SEEKING SARAH

"Billingsley has written another engrossing page-turner about a complicated mother-daughter relationship that readers will enjoy into the wee hours."

—*Library Journal* (starred review)

THE PERFECT MISTRESS

"Billingsley is skilled at making flawed characters sympathetic, even as they meet painful justice."

—*Booklist*

"I advise you to hold on to your books or e-readers. You are in for one heck of a ride."

—*Romance in Color*

MAMA'S BOY

One of Library Journal's *Best Books of 2015*

"This is an outstanding story that handles every mother's nightmare from multiple views while addressing one of society's deepest controversies. The end was like watching a cliffhanger that one did not see coming!"

—*RT Book Reviews*

WHAT'S DONE IN THE DARK

"An entertaining book with suspense, drama, and a little humor . . . The twists and turns will have readers rushing to turn the pages."

—*Authors & Readers Book Corner*

THE SECRET SHE KEPT

"Entertaining and riveting . . . Heartfelt and realistic . . . A must-read."

—*AAM Book Club*

HOLY ROLLERS

"Sensational . . . [Billingsley] makes you fall in love with these characters."

—RT Book Reviews

THE DEVIL IS A LIE

"A romantic page-turner dipped in heavenly goodness."

—RT Book Reviews (4½ stars)

"Fast-moving and hilarious."

—Publishers Weekly

CAN I GET A WITNESS?

A USA Today 2007 Summer Sizzler

"An emotional ride."

—Ebony

"Billingsley serves up a humdinger of a plot."

—Essence

THE PASTOR'S WIFE

"Billingsley has done it again. . . . A true page-turner."

—Urban Reviews

I KNOW I'VE BEEN CHANGED

#1 Dallas Morning News bestseller

"Grabs you from the first page and never lets go . . . Bravo!"

—Victoria Christopher Murray

A LITTLE BIT OF
Karma

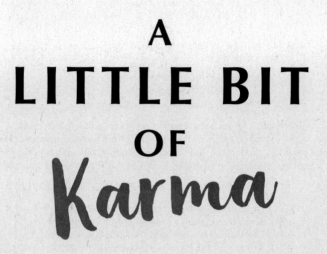

ReShonda Tate Billingsley

GALLERY BOOKS

New York   London   Toronto   Sydney   New Delhi

Gallery Books
An Imprint of Simon & Schuster, Inc.
1230 Avenue of the Americas
New York, NY 10020

First Gallery Books trade paperback edition September 2020

GALLERY BOOKS and colophon are
registered trademarks of Simon & Schuster, Inc.

For information about special discounts for bulk purchases,
please contact Simon & Schuster Special Sales at 1-866-506-1949
or business@simonandschuster.com.

The Simon & Schuster Speakers Bureau can bring authors
to your live event. For more information or to book an event,
contact the Simon & Schuster Speakers Bureau at 1-866-248-3049
or visit our website at www.simonspeakers.com.

Manufactured in the United States of America

1 3 5 7 9 10 8 6 4 2

Library of Congress Cataloging-in-Publication Data

Names: Billingsley, ReShonda Tate, author.
Title: A little bit of karma : a novel / ReShonda Tate Billingsley.
Description: First edition. | New York : Gallery Books, 2020.
Identifiers: LCCN 2020019993 | ISBN 9781439183588 (paperback) | ISBN
9781439183687 (ebook)
Subjects: GSAFD: Romantic suspense fiction.
Classification: LCC PS3602.I445 L58 2020 | DDC 813/.6—dc23
LC record available at https://lccn.loc.gov/2020019993

ISBN 978-1-4391-8358-8
ISBN 978-1-4391-8368-7 (ebook)

A
LITTLE BIT
OF
Karma

one

My life was a lie. One of those whoppers that should've been a special at Burger King.

But my best friend/producer was once again reminding me that I was being paid extremely well for this lie. Nicole Dunbar had been the producer of our hit radio show, *Love with the Lovejoys*, since my husband, Jay, and I had started it two years ago. That, coupled with the fact that we'd been best friends since our days at Howard University, gave her a front-row seat to the problems in my marriage. In fact, it was Nicole who had told me from the very beginning that the charming personality I found so endearing back when Jay and I first met would one day aggravate me to no end.

Truer words have never been uttered.

"I bet it was one of those women he was always flirting with," I muttered as I paced back and forth in the holding room. We were in the conference room at the newly remodeled Buccaneer Hotel, preparing for a weeklong retreat that I had no desire to be a part of. Granted, I'd been gung-ho when the organizers first pitched this retreat to us, billed as a one-of-a-kind event at which attendees could reconnect and rediscover love. Jay and I were set to be keynote speakers and lead several workshops in intimate settings. I'd been excited about it. But that was before I knew that my husband was a cheating bastard.

Before I knew my marriage was a whopper of a lie.

"Come on, don't go down that road. You're going to work yourself up into a tizzy," Nicole said. She was sitting at a table, reviewing some of the logistical paperwork for the conference.

"I just don't want to see him," I finally admitted, walking over to the window to gaze out at the beautiful scenery.

"It's not that hard," Nicole replied.

That was easy for her to say. Her "for better" wasn't at its worst.

I turned to face my friend. "Seven years, Nicole," I said. "Jay threw away seven years and a lucrative career over some woman, but I'm supposed to just smile like everything is okay." I grabbed a small bottled water from the ice bucket before resuming my pacing.

She put her pen down and gave me her undivided attention. "Yes. When you're getting paid a half-million dollars, yes, you smile like you guys are . . ." She paused, like she was thinking. "Um . . ."

I flicked my hand in exasperation. "Exactly. You can't name one married couple as an example of amazing love."

She snapped her fingers. "Like Barack and Michelle."

I rolled my eyes. "Girl, Jay can't carry Barack's water."

"Tell that to someone who doesn't know how in love with him you are," she said.

"Were. Past tense." I gulped the water and tossed the empty bottle. I didn't know if it was my nerves that had me feeling dehydrated or if I was just that thirsty.

Nicole waved me off. "Look, we do not have time to re-hash the infidelity of Jay Lovejoy. You agreed to do this con-ference, more than three thousand people are registered, and we have a contract to uphold. Now, they want a happy cou-ple: we need to deliver a happy couple to them."

I watched as a large truck backed up to the loading dock. They were no doubt bringing items for the retreat.

"Shan, you can do this," Nicole said.

I knew my best friend was right. It had been five weeks since I'd discovered my husband was having an affair. It had been the most difficult thing I'd ever endured. Everyone around us was concerned about the Lovejoy franchise—the syndicated radio show, the bestselling books, the hundreds of thousands of social media followers—everything that made us what *Essence* magazine called "The Couple of the Century." We'd built our Lovejoy brand on how in love we were. How we'd managed to have it all and keep the love and the joy alive in our relationship. And it was all a lie. In this moment, in this space, in this heartache, I didn't care about any of that. I only wanted to repair the hole that was now in my heart.

I'd made Jay move out the day that I'd discovered the affair, and the plan had been to cut him out of my life. But that was proving much harder than I'd ever imagined.

Nicole eased up behind me and rubbed my back. "Shannon, you have been kicking butt and taking names since I met you our freshman year of college. This is just another obstacle that you will overcome."

That brought a slight smile to my face. "Yeah, Howard wasn't ready for me." I was one of those overachieving students who was a student leader and a straight-A student my first semester on campus.

"Exactly," Nicole said. "So I need you to summon up that same strength, put on your game face, and do this."

My shoulders slumped as I stared outside. This really was a beautiful place.

When I didn't move, Nicole came around in front of me. Her eyes bore into mine, like she was trying to use X-ray vision to see into my soul—and the real reason I didn't want to be here.

"You didn't talk to him, did you?" she asked.

When I didn't answer, she sighed. "I thought you guys met to talk so this wouldn't be the first time you'd seen each other in the past month."

"I didn't go."

"What?" Nicole exclaimed.

I looked down. When I looked up, my eyes were misty. Nicole was the only one I allowed to see my vulnerable side. With her, I didn't need to pretend. With her, I could show how much Jay's betrayal really hurt.

"I didn't want to see him." I swallowed the lump in my throat. "I wasn't ready to see him." The day that I'd confronted Jay—and he'd confessed—I'd put him out. And although he'd tried multiple times to talk to me about it, I'd told him I had nothing to say. He'd admitted it. A "why" didn't matter. And since he wouldn't give me details, there was no need to talk.

I expected Nicole to put on her producer hat and chastise me, but she stayed in best-friend mode.

"Awww, sweetie, I get it." She patted the tear that had managed to seep out. "But no more running. You have to face him now. Get through this retreat, finalize the divorce, and then pick up the pieces of your life."

I sighed. Nicole was right. I needed to just release this fear and face my soon-to-be ex. "Fine, but don't expect me to be nice," I said.

"No, ma'am," Nicole said. "You can't walk around here all week acting all funky and wearing an attitude on your shoulder. Remember, Quincy said we have to give the people what they came for."

I huffed. "I'm sorry. I'm not a skilled liar like Jay. It's not easy for me to pretend like my soon-to-be ex-husband is the greatest thing since sliced bread, especially when I know that he's not."

The door to the greenroom opened and Tara, the conference coordinator, walked in.

"Good afternoon, Mrs. Lovejoy. Welcome to the Virgin Islands. How was your flight?" Tara asked.

"Hi, Tara. It was fine." I managed a smile.

Tara handed me an envelope. "Wonderful. I have both you and Mr. Lovejoy checked into the presidential suite. Your bags will be delivered up to your room when they arrive."

"Tara, umm . . ." I weighed how to get my next statement out. Aside from Nicole and Quincy, no one knew anything about my problems with Jay, and separate rooms would only fuel speculation. But I couldn't bear the thought of spending the whole week in the same room as him. "I was just wondering if . . . you thought . . . well, is there any way to get Jay a separate room? It's just . . . we need . . ." I couldn't even think of a good lie. I stopped as Nicole waved her hand.

"Tara, if you don't mind, let me talk with Shannon, please?" Nicole said.

Tara looked confused. "Well, ummm, do you want me to try to get another room?" she asked me. "That might be difficult, but, um, I . . . I can see what I can do."

Nicole shook her head, answering for me. "That won't be necessary." She chuckled. "Jay has a horrible snoring problem and Dr. Shannon was joking about wanting to get a good night's sleep. If you can just make sure their bags get taken up, that would be great."

Tara nodded before scurrying off. I groaned as I glared at my friend. Nicole glared right back. "I thought you were going to behave yourself," she said.

"I am. But that doesn't mean I have to stay in the room with him the whole week." I knew I was acting like a pouty brat, but I was hurting, and the fact that I had to mask that pain only exacerbated the problem.

"Number one, the hotel is booked to capacity," Nicole said. "Trying to find another room would be nearly impossible. Not to mention, it would raise a lot of eyebrows." She held up two fingers. "Number two, the suite you're in has two bedrooms. Just put him in one and you take the other. And number three, and most important, I thought we had this discussion before we left D.C. There is too much at stake here. You've got hundreds of thousands of dollars on the line here, and unless you're prepared to write a check to pay the Family First Foundation, I suggest you get to faking it."

I folded my arms across my chest as I stared out the window. Jay had arrived and had barely stepped out of the SUV when he was swarmed by women. My husband was a popular nineties R&B singer who had retained a loyal following. I watched the way they were swooning, jockeying for position near him. And as usual, Jay was being charismatic and had the women giggling like schoolgirls. I saw him laughing with a group of them by the front door. "It's going to take a whole lot more than faking it," I said, watching as some woman seductively touched Jay's chest. "It's going to take an Academy Award–winning performance to make it through this week."

Nicole glanced out at Jay, then back at me. "Then I suggest you get to acting, Viola."

two

My husband and I were face-to-face for the first time in five weeks. And it felt like five years.

"Hello, Shannon," Jay said as he walked into the holding room.

"Jay" was all I could reply. In this moment, I hated this man with everything inside me. But damn, he was still so fine. Right now, he was in his usual stylish attire—a camel-colored jacket, a black mock turtleneck, and black slacks. And, of course, his passion: Italian-imported loafers.

I immediately noticed that his dimple was gone. Just moments ago, Jay had been smiling at the group of women outside. Now his face bore a look of disdain. That was laughable, since he was the one who had cheated.

"Jay, so glad that you made it in okay," Nicole said, stepping in to ease the tension that hung in the air.

"Thanks, Nicole," he said, finally smiling.

"Let me go check to see if the driver is ready to take you guys to the radio station," Nicole said.

Jay walked over to grab a bottled water. I suddenly became interested in the pattern of the ceramic tile.

"How have you been, Shannon?" he asked.

"How do you think?" I replied. I might be forced to fake it out in public, but in private, I wasn't about to pretend.

He sighed. "Shannon, we really should talk."

"We have nothing to talk about. You admitted to the affair. And then you had the audacity to not want to give me details." I glared at him. It was bad enough that he'd cheated, but no matter how much I demanded details, he wouldn't oblige. I think that's what took my fury to a whole other level.

"Because I don't think the details will help anything," he said.

"They could've helped me! Regardless, you were the one in the wrong. You don't get to make the decision about what I needed."

Though we hadn't seen each other since we'd taped our radio show five weeks ago, we'd been communicating via text. First, he'd just kept trying to call and apologize. But if he couldn't answer my questions, I couldn't be bothered with his apologies. Finally, when I wouldn't engage with him over the phone, he'd shifted to daily texts trying to salvage the radio show, the second book of our two-book deal, and this retreat.

"Look, I don't want to fight with you. I know what's at stake, so I'm ready to make sure everyone has a good time," he said, almost like he was trying to give me a verbal reminder.

Nicole stepped back inside. "Okay, the driver is ready. They said people are already lining up at the bookstore."

Jay continued to stare at me until I broke away. "Fine," I said, slipping my sunglasses on. "Let the show begin."

The three of us walked outside, where word must've spread about our arrival, because several more people were there, waiting around for autographs.

"We are so sorry: the Lovejoys must get to their radio remote," Nicole told the people as they called out to us and thrust papers and books at us to sign. "Please join them this evening at Delphi Books for their book signing to kick off the retreat."

She motioned for us to continue down the walkway. The touch of Jay's hand jolted me, and I glanced down in shock as he took my hand and led me over to the SUV. But then I saw why as a photographer flashed his camera in front of us. At that moment, I was grateful I hadn't removed my sunglasses, because I would have hated for anyone to see the pain in my eyes.

"Sorry about that," the driver said, shooing the photographer away. "As you can imagine, your retreat has been the talk of the island."

"That's a good thing," Jay said as we climbed inside the black Escalade.

"I'll see you guys over there," Nicole said. "I'll catch a taxi after I make sure the crew have everything they need."

The driver made sure we were safely in the SUV and darted back around to the driver's side. Once we had pulled off and were on our way, he glanced in his rearview mirror. "Mr. Lovejoy, can I just say, I'm a huge fan. I actually proposed to my lady while one of your songs played. I love your voice."

Jay flashed a genuine smile. "Thank you so much. And call me Jay."

I rolled my eyes and stared out the window. That melodic voice had been Jay's signature on our popular Washington, D.C.–based call-in radio show. It had been his claim to fame since the nineties, when he'd burst onto the scene as a fresh-faced R&B crooner with the voice of Barry White. It didn't hurt now that at one time Jay had been one of the hottest R&B singers on the market. He was all the DeBarge brothers, Jamie Foxx, and Ginuwine rolled up into one. And then, he had the looks to go along with every lonely woman's fantasy. He was the caring, sympathetic one, the one women secretly dreamed they could call their own. I had often joked with Jay that he presented an image for all these lonely women of a devoted, romantic man who would cater to their every need. I was the noted psychologist, the hard-nosed dose of reality who urged the women to put on their big-girl panties and get their lives back together.

For a while, we seemed like the perfect team. Until my husband decided that our lives weren't good enough.

"Did you stop and pick up food?"

"Dang, can you say hello?"

I looked up from my laptop and glanced at my husband. I took a deep breath and decided to try again. All we'd been doing was fighting for the past six months and I was tired of it. "I'm sorry," I said. "Hello. How was your meeting?"

He tossed his keys and cell phone on the bar. "It was fine. Quincy is finalizing all the details with the foundation. They're excited about the retreat. By the way, they wired the money to our account. I'll transfer it to our savings." He paused and looked at me. "Unless you want your half sent to your own account."

My immediate reaction was to say "Of course." But since that had become just one of the main sources of contention with us lately, I just left it alone.

"That's fine."

We stared at each other like we didn't know what to say to one another—a far cry from the way we used to be.

Finally, he said, "Well, I'll call DoorDash and have something delivered. I'm going to take a shower."

As he turned to walk away, it suddenly dawned on me that I couldn't remember the last time Jay had kissed me. We were still having sex, but it was like we fulfilled our carnal desires and then went our separate ways.

I needed wine. I walked over to the bar, grabbed the bottle of pinot grigio and a glass. As I was pouring the wine, Jay's cell phone rang. I glanced at it and saw Quincy's Work flash across the screen. He probably had questions about the negotiations. I usually let Jay handle that part of our partnership; I took a sip of the wine and then headed upstairs with his phone in my hand.

I was halfway up the stairs when a text message dinged from Quincy's number. The cleavage shot caused me to stop in my *tracks. I couldn't see the whole picture, but the next message that came in caused me to lean against the side of the railing to keep from falling.*

> Today was amazing. I will be dreaming about you inside me all night. I love you.

Why would Quincy be sending that message to Jay? Maybe he was showing Jay a message from one of the many women he dated. But my gut wasn't buying that explanation. So I did something I'd never done: I entered Jay's passcode (he kept the same one for everything) to open his phone.

Though the contact info said Quincy's Work, *that was obviously a cover-up. Message after message revealed the lie that was my life. My husband was having an affair and this woman was in love.*

I couldn't contain my breath; my head seemed to be spinning. I glanced up at the top of the staircase to see my husband staring at me in shock.

———

Unlike a lot of men, Jay hadn't tried to lie his way out of that situation. Oh, he'd been shocked silent for a moment, then extremely remorseful. But he'd come clean—somewhat, anyway, confessing to the affair, though he'd sworn that he didn't know why she was saying "I love you," because he wasn't in love with her.

I shook away thoughts of that painful past and tried to focus on the present.

The drive to the station took about twenty minutes. Jay tried to make idle chitchat about the beautiful scenery. Had this been another time, another place, I would've snuggled up to him and savored every word. Instead, I ignored everything he said. I had to—it was the only way I'd be able to get through the rest of the week.

"Look," Jay said as we pulled up to the radio station. His voice was filled with exasperation because he'd tried to talk to me the entire ride and I'd refused to engage him. "I realize things are rough between us, but we're both professionals. Can you put aside your anger for the time being so we can do this?"

I was sick of people acting like I could just extract my pain and set it on a shelf or something.

"Whatever, Jay," I said, waving him off.

He sighed and stepped out of his side of the vehicle. It was heartbreaking to watch our demise. *Vanity Fair* had dubbed us a "power couple of the new millennium." The *New York Times* had written that our new book, *Real Talk*, was "the ultimate guide to getting your marriage back on track," and just last month, we'd gotten an offer to take our relationship advice to reality TV.

Yet our whole life was now a lie. That thought made me cry inside.

three

There's nothing worse than a whining woman. On second thought, yes, there is: a woman whining over a worthless man. And this caller had all boxes checked. I already hadn't wanted to do this remote show, but the foundation had billed it as one of the features for those who couldn't attend, so it wasn't like I had much choice.

"I just want him to love me," the woman on the phone cried. "Why won't he love me?"

I was in full feminist mode and wanted to reach through the phone and slap some sense into this woman. I'd seen my share of foolish women, but I would never understand why women would continue to shed tears over a no-good man. This was exactly why I did radio and not television, because I had the hardest time masking my disdain. It was also why I refused to give Jay another chance. A cheating leopard didn't change his spots.

"Come on, sweetheart. It's not that bad." There went my

husband's soothing voice. He was doing what he did best—using his Barry White, I-can-seduce-any-woman-I-want voice to calm some heartbroken woman. "He's not worth your tears."

"But he said he loved me," the caller whined in her thick accent. "I forgave him after the first outside child. Now this woman is having twins. What am I supposed to do?"

I shook my head. All of these callers were from the area. I guessed cheating was universal.

"Oh, give me a break." I hadn't even realized that I'd said that out loud until Jay bugged his eyes in my direction.

"What Dr. Shannon meant to say," Jay quickly said, "is that only you can determine your worth. If he can't recognize the diamond that you are, that's his loss. You know our tagline with *Love with the Lovejoys*?"

"One man's trash is another man's treasure?" The woman sniffed.

"Yes, and a woman must know her worth, then add tax," Jay added.

I fought back the urge to yell, "Enough, already! This hypocrite is the last person to be dishing out advice!"

It wasn't that I was a hard-core feminist, I just thought it was useless to waste time and energy on a man who treated you like crap. And half the female callers to our syndicated radio show were in one-way relationships, with them trying desperately to get the man to "do right."

I usually zoned out when Jay got into his "crisis comforting" mode, so I started counting down the seconds until this conference wrapped. It took me only about two minutes to calculate that it would be 604,220 seconds before this night-mare was over.

I refocused on the caller when I heard Jay say, "So you call us anytime, beautiful."

"You can't even see me," the woman said, her voice soft. I could feel her smile through the phone.

"I see your spirit and there is beauty in that. I just want you to see it too," Jay replied.

"Thank you so much, Jay." The woman sniffed again. "You always know what to say to make a lady feel better. We are so glad you're here and I can't wait to meet you in person."

"Well, make sure you come up to me and personally say hello," Jay said.

I rolled my eyes as Jay disconnected the call and tossed to the break.

When we'd started this show, we'd joked about how empa-thetic Jay was with the women. But we'd quickly discovered that that was a major selling point to the show, so I'd learned to live with it. If I had only known then what I knew now.

Jay didn't say anything to me—just busied himself on the phone until the "on-air" light came back on.

"Welcome back to all our lovely *Lovejoy* listeners," Jay said. "Let's take our last call of the evening."

He motioned for the sound engineer to patch the call through and looked at the pop-up message on the computer screen. "I understand we have Sheryl on the line. How are you doing, Sheryl? Are you giving good love?" he said. I found myself wondering if I would ever get "good love" again.

Sheryl giggled through the phone. "I wish. Maybe if I had a man like you, I'd get some good lovin'."

Jay glanced over at me and I didn't bother to hide my agitation.

"Well, if I were single, I just might have to give it to you," he joked back. "But you know, I have my lovely wife here in the studio, and I don't think she'd go for that."

I wanted to lean in and let Sheryl know that Jay would in fact soon be single. This was probably the bimbo he was screwing anyway. I think that was part of my torture. I didn't know who she was, and for the past five weeks everyone—from the cleaning lady to the barista at Starbucks—had been suspect. He owed me an explanation, even if we were splitting up. You don't throw away all these years for no reason. But I wasn't going to beg, so we'd drifted into the world of silence where we now resided.

"Oh, no disrespect, Dr. Shannon," Sheryl said, interrupting my thoughts. "I was just teasing Jay."

Nicole peered at me through the studio window, and I knew she was sending me a mental note to just "shake it off."

I plastered a smile on and leaned in. "No disrespect taken, Sheryl. A lot of women would love to get good lovin' from my husband," I said, my sarcasm on full throttle.

"But you're lucky, because I can hear it in his voice: he only has eyes for you," Sheryl replied.

Then you can't hear, I wanted to say. Instead, I just sneered across the table, "Yeah, that's my husband, Jay Lovejoy. I'm just so lucky to have him."

Jay quickly jumped back in the conversation. "So tell us, Sheryl, how can the Lovejoys help you out this evening?"

Sheryl sighed and the joy left her voice. "Well, my husband has fallen out of love with me, and I need some advice on how I can get him back," she said.

I couldn't help but smile as I leaned back in my chair, folded my arms, and smirked. I couldn't wait to hear Jay answer this one. Since he wouldn't talk to me about why he'd fallen out of love (because he had to have fallen out of love in order to cheat in the first place).

Maybe I could get some insight into his mindset from his answer to Sheryl.

Jay glanced over at me as if he wanted me to answer. I raised an eyebrow to let him know the floor was all his.

"Well, ahem . . ." Jay cleared his throat. The way he squirmed, it was obvious he was uncomfortable. "How do you know he's fallen out of love?"

"Let's see, maybe it was when he became someone I didn't know," Sheryl continued. "Or maybe it's because he won't touch me. He acts like I repulse him. Or maybe it was when he moved out. Or maybe it was when he introduced my kids to his mistress."

Oh, this just keeps getting better, I thought, shifting in the chair to get comfortable. My expression let Jay know I had no intention of joining in this conversation.

Jay ignored Nicole and the sound engineer, who were also staring like they were in the middle of a good soap opera.

"My friends say I should just let him go, but I just thought, you know, you and Dr. Shannon are always talking about how couples give up too quickly. I just want to know if it's worth fighting for."

Jay deliberately didn't look my way. "Well, Sheryl, only you can answer whether your relationship is worth fighting for, but if his feelings for you have changed, there's not much you can do about it."

"But I think outside forces, namely that slut he's sleeping with, are clouding his judgment," Sheryl protested. "I know he loves me. It's just that we were having money problems, and the stress of everything wore us both down. If I know that, I'm supposed to just let him go? I'm supposed to let her win and give her my life?" She sounded frustrated and on the verge of hysteria. "Dr. Shannon, what do you think? Don't you want to weigh in?" Sheryl asked.

I leaned into the mic. "Nope, Jay's handling this just fine." I leaned back and continued to stare at my husband.

He blew a frustrated breath but continued talking. "Sheryl, all I can tell you is that you can't make a man love you. But only you can make the call about whether what he feels for this other woman is real or just something on the side. I will tell you this: for a lot of people, when the love is gone, it's gone. And there's nothing you can do to get it back."

The smirk drifted from my face. Jay's words felt like a knife through my heart. Was it gone for him that bad? Was that why he was unfaithful? How had we gotten to this place, and how had I not seen it coming? Was I so consumed with my anger and resentment that I hadn't noticed my husband fell out of love with me?

"So you think I should just let him go?" Sheryl sounded like her voice was cracking.

"Sadly, that's my advice. Let him go," Jay said softly. Our crew was shocked. Jay never advised callers to walk away without a fight.

"It doesn't mean that he didn't love you. It just means something has changed and he is no longer in love with you. But that just means there's something better out there for you," Jay added.

Sheryl inhaled. "Dr. Shannon, do you agree?" she asked, her voice quivering like that was not the advice she'd expected.

I didn't answer, and after a few seconds of dead air (an eternity in radio), Jay leaned into the mic. "So sorry, Sheryl. I wish we could continue, but our time is up. Thank you for calling, and we wish you all the best." He cut his eyes at me as he disconnected her call and continued talking. "As you may know, we are broadcasting live from the Virgin Islands, where we are all week for our Lovejoy Retreat. If you're on your way, we can't wait to see you. To all our Lovejoy listeners, enjoy the last of our best-of shows, and we'll be back on your radio dials soon." He paused and our eyes met. "Until then . . . keep some joy in your love and a light in your life."

Normally, this would have been where I leaned in and, with the ease of a seasoned professional, delivered our closing line: "Thank you for getting love on the line. Until next time, make sure you live, laugh, and love."

But since I hadn't laughed in months, my love was destroyed, and my life ruined, all I could do was remain silent.

The sound engineer must've known I had zoned out, because he potted up the theme music and Jay and I both simultaneously removed our headphones.

"Just once, can you try being a little sympathetic to our callers?" He tossed his headphones down on the desk in disgust.

It was amazing how he always found something to get irritated with me about. Even before I'd asked for a divorce, he'd always been irritated—probably his way of trying to cover up his affair. The microphone was off, so pretending time was over.

"That's your job, Mr. I-Always-Know-How-to-Make-a-Woman-Feel-Better," I said, finally finding the voice that had escaped me. I should've known that a fight would ensue after that last caller. For the past few months, a fight had *always* been ensuing whenever we were around each other.

Jay just stared at me. "When did you turn into a bitter old woman?" he asked.

My left eyebrow shot up. "*Old?*" I'd give him a pass on the "bitter," since he knew there was a basis for my bitterness, but I was barely thirty-eight, so I wasn't about to let the "old" comment slide.

I stood, tossing my scripts into the trash can. "Maybe I'm just sick and tired of watching you flirt with these damn women right under my nose," I snapped. "Maybe that caller is the whore you're screwing."

Jay sighed, then shook his head as he stood as well and gathered up his papers. "I'm not doing this with you."

I didn't know why he would even try to pick that fight with me. He knew I would never change my mind about sniveling, despondent women. Six months into our radio show, I'd wanted to bail for that very reason. I preferred private practice because with the caliber of clients I had, they might have had issues, but they weren't whiny women. Maybe I'd go back into private practice now that my life had done a 180. I could still write my own books and maybe even do the speaking circuit.

Before I could reply, the door to the studio swung open. "Sorry I missed the show close," Nicole said as she walked into the studio. "I had to do something with the conference coordinator." She stopped when she felt the tension in the room. She looked at Jay and then at me. Then she shook her head. "Good grief. How did you two get into a fight that fast?" she asked. "We've only been off the air a few minutes."

"It's nothing," Jay said.

I sighed and flicked my hand. "Same story. Different day."

"Yep. The story of our life," Jay muttered, glaring at me.

"Look, I'd love to moderate this argument/discussion/ nothing, again, but we don't have time," Nicole said, motioning toward the clock. "You have to get over to the bookstore. That pesky publicist has already called here twice trying to make sure you were on your way. The signing is in thirty minutes."

"Fine." Jay headed toward the door.

"Can you guys just please play nice?" Nicole asked as he passed her.

The two of us exchanged glances, though neither bothered to answer. We both knew playing nice would be a whole lot easier said than done.

four

The sounds of Anita Baker filled the black SUV as Jay and I rode to the bookstore. The last thing I felt like doing was going to a book signing and faking the funk like all was perfect in my world. Or even worse, having people looking at me with pity. Though the media hadn't gotten wind of the affair, there'd been some rumblings after some obscure gossip site posted a line item about there being "trouble in paradise for the Lovejoys." I knew it was just a matter of time.

I glanced over at my soon-to-be ex and instantly cursed the fluttering in my heart. After all this time, after all this pain, that man could still ignite a flame in my soul. But I guess that was understandable. The moment we'd met, our connection had been instant. I leaned back on the headrest as my mind traveled back to that day.

"Hey, here's a novel idea, why don't you stop reading the book and participate? This is for charity, you know."

I rolled my eyes at my best friend and dropped the stack of papers back in my briefcase.

"When my editor cancels my book deal because I missed my deadline, I'm coming to live with you," I said.

Nicole huffed as she ran her fingers through her natural tresses. "You work on that manuscript nonstop. Taking a few hours off won't kill you. You ought to be tired of writing that clinical stuff anyway."

"It's not clinical. It's self-help." This was my second published work with the American Psychiatric Association. The first had been on mental health. For my field, my first book had done exceptionally well. This one was on the complexities of relationships. Between my practice and what I'd inherited from my absent father upon his death, I was pretty well off financially.

"Whatever, I need some steamy, hot love scenes," Nicole replied. "But seeing as how you haven't had any steamy, hot sex in a year, you probably don't even know how to write those." She slid a glass toward me across the high-top bar table. "Drink, and let's have fun. You have got to do better."

"Look, you wanted me to get out the house. I'm out the house." I folded my arms and leaned back on my barstool.

"It's been a year since Eddie broke it off. You need to get out and enjoy yourself."

I looked around the room. There had to be two hundred people here at the Hilton, most of them desperate-looking women. "And a charity auction event is the place to get out and enjoy myself?"

"Yes. They have some fine men being bid on."

I took a sip of my drink, then set it back down. "First of all, slavery is illegal. Secondly, I'm not that desperate where I have to

buy a man, and I'm sure not competing with another woman trying to buy one." I slid my auction paddle toward Nicole. "So here,
it's all yours."

Nicole ignored me as she opened the auction booklet. "Look,
they have an NFL player," she squealed.

"Dog."

"The TV anchor from Channel 11."

"He's gay. His boyfriend does my hair."

She tapped another photo. "Okay, what about this guy? He's an
investment banker."

"He looks shysty."

"You don't know anything about these men," Nicole huffed.

"And I have no desire to." I sipped some more of my martini. I
was so over all of this.

"So you're just going to be an old maid? I don't think so. You can
try to act like you don't care about having a man and kids, but I
know better."

"It's all overrated."

"You just haven't found the right one. We both know how much
you're itching to have kids." Nicole flipped through the auction
book again. "Oooh."

"Oooh, what?" I said, leaning over her shoulder.

"Oooh, him." Nicole pointed to the stage as the mistress of cere-
monies returned from the intermission.

"Now, I know we'll get top dollar for this one," the emcee began.

"This so reminds me of a slave block," I said, shaking my head
and leaning back in my seat. "Where's the ACLU or NAACP when
you need them?"

"Don't be ridiculous." Nicole pushed my shoulder. "It's all in fun. It's a charity auction."

"It feels rather pimpish to me."

The emcee leaned into the mic, a huge grin across her face. "You knew him for his hits 'I Don't Want to Be Alone' and 'Touch My Insides.'"

The crowd instantly started screaming. I leaned forward and squinted, since it was hard to see from our seats.

"Is that Jay Lovejoy?" I asked.

"The one and only," Nicole said, pointing to his picture in the booklet. "That's who you need to be bidding on."

I flicked my hand. "Girl, please. Do you see all these women around this room ready to throw their panties at him, even though he hasn't had a hit in fifteen years?"

"I heard he invested his money wisely. He had several restaurants."

"Well, it wasn't too wise because, like you said, the operative word is had. Last I heard, he was penniless," I replied.

"Well, I don't know the man's personal finances. I just know he is personally fine." Nicole licked her lips to punctuate her admiration.

I'd have to cosign with her on that, though, because Jay Lovejoy might have been on the scene for more than twenty years, but he still had that youthful sex appeal.

The emcee strutted over to Jay; he took her hand, then kissed it, and the crowd went wild.

"Are you sure I can't keep this one for myself?" the emcee joked to the crowd as nos resonated through the room.

She laughed and turned back to face the excited crowd. "I guess that means one of you will be the lucky one tonight. Ladies, who's going to give me top dollar for Jay Lovejoy? Starting bid is two thousand dollars."

"You have got to be kidding me," I muttered, shaking my head. Apparently, I was the only one not enjoying the show, though, as the room lit up with screams and catcalls. I reached down for my briefcase and pulled my manuscript back out.

I tuned the emcee out until I heard: "We're at five thousand dollars; can I get fifty-five hundred?" The woman rambled off the number in an auctioneer's voice before saying, "Ladies, this is Jay 'Three Number One Hits' Lovejoy; I know I can get fifty-five hundred dollars for the babies in Haiti."

The chatter continued. Nicole was so into it that she hadn't even noticed that I had resumed working.

"Y'all would make such cute babies," Nicole swooned.

"Whatever, Nicole." I didn't look up from my manuscript. I knew I should've stayed home and finished this. It was due a week ago and I'd promised my editor that I'd have it done by Monday. That left three days to get this finished, and here I was, at this degrading auction.

I was just about to circle an error I'd caught when, out of the corner of my eye, I saw Nicole raise her paddle and shout, "Ten thousand dollars!"

Several gasps filled the room.

"Are you crazy?" I whispered.

"Ten thousand dollars to the lady in the corner, number forty-two," the emcee said, excitement filling her voice.

Nicole giggled.

"Why in the world would you do that? You don't have that kind of mone . . ." My words trailed off as reality hit me. "Number forty-two is my paddle!"

Nicole doubled over in laughter, like she found this hilarious. I did not. "You don't have ten thousand dollars!"

"But you do! You were just complaining that you needed some tax write-offs for that book deal." She turned her attention back to the stage. "And there he is, Mr. Schedule C Deduction."

"Sold to number forty-two. Mr. Lovejoy, go meet your date for the evening."

My heart went into acrobatic mode as Jay sauntered over to my table with a swagger like Denzel Washington and Barack Obama rolled into one.

"Well, I would say I'm honored," Jay said, his eyes never leaving mine, "but this is nothing but a blessing. My boys were so sure I would end up being auctioned off to some hard-on-the-eyes lonely heart."

"Well, as you can see, my friend is far from hard on the eyes," Nicole interjected.

"I know," he replied. "Wow. Has anyone ever told you that you look like—"

I gathered my words and finished his sentence. "Vanessa L. Williams, the former Miss America? Yes, all the time."

Jay looked confused. "No, actually, I was going to say the lady from the Mrs. Butterworth commercial."

My mouth gaped, as I was unsure how to respond.

"I'm kidding," he quickly added, laughing. "I was going to say Vanessa, but I didn't want to come off as lame."

"And you didn't think the Mrs. Butterworth comment was lame?" I replied.

"Touché." He chuckled, then stuck out his hand to shake mine. "Jay Lovejoy, at your service, ready to serve you, madam."

Nicole leaned in over the table. "Ready to serve her . . . how, exactly?"

I pushed my friend's shoulder. "Nicole!"

Jay laughed. "For now . . . in strictly PG ways. But who knows what the future holds?"

"Her future needs to hold some rated-XXX ways," Nicole said with a wicked grin.

"Oh my God!" I shook my head as I looked at Jay. "Please excuse my friend." I paused. This man's eyes were enchanting, like they could suck out your soul. I shook myself out of my momentary trance. "Ummm, she's just . . ." Why the hell couldn't I find my words?

Jay smiled. "It's all good. Those are the types of friends we need in our lives. Ones who keep it real."

"Oh, and I keep it real real." Nicole stood. "But my girl paid good money for your time, so I'm going to let you two have at it." She hugged me. "Shannon, relax, enjoy yourself. You need it."

"Nicole, you can't leave me," I said when she released me.

"Mr. Lovejoy will make sure you get home." She smiled at him, and he nodded his agreement.

I jumped up and grabbed her as she was walking out. "I don't know this dude like that. He could be a serial killer," I whispered.

"Girl, that man is a superstar. Or was a superstar. Trust, he isn't trying to kill you. He's fine, charismatic, and shoot, worst case, just have him sing to you all night." She glanced at Jay over my shoulder. "Goodbye, Jay. I look forward to seeing you again soon."

"You will," he said.

Nicole looked back at me and nodded. "I like him."

"Nicole."

"Bye, girl!" she said.

I wanted to run after her, scream about how she was violating every girl code under the sun. But my feet were frozen, until Jay eased up behind me and said, "I left my butcher knife at home, so you're safe from the possible serial killer tonight."

I slowly turned around. "Umm, ahh . . ."

He smiled. "It's fine. Let's just sit here and talk. Part of this whole charity thing is that you get me for one date. We can have that date right here. Just sitting and talking for a bit. And afterward, if you're ready to forget you ever met me, cool. And the little kids in Haiti will still come out winners."

There was something about his voice that soothed me, and I instantly felt myself relax. "Sorry," I said, sliding back into my seat. "This . . . this just isn't really my thing."

"Mine either, trust me. I only did this as a favor to the organizer," he said, before calling the waiter over to order more drinks.

It was five in the morning on Saturday when it dawned on me that I had completely forgotten about my manuscript. We had sat and talked at the hotel until the custodial staff gave us the side eye; then we'd had breakfast on the Navy Pier, gone our separate ways, and been back together by dinner.

And we had been inseparable ever since.

The memory of how Jay and I had met brought a pang to my heart, especially in light of where we were now.

I glanced at my watch. We'd been riding for fifteen minutes. Jay sat in the back seat next to me, engrossed in his phone. I couldn't take the silence anymore.

I raised the divider window so the driver couldn't hear our conversation. "So I guess you're just not going to say anything?" I asked.

Jay released a heavy sigh. "What is there to say, Shannon?" He looked up at me, exasperation written all over his face. "You're the one who said you didn't want to talk to me. I'm tired of fighting with you. That's all we do, fight."

"I wonder why," I said, rolling my eyes as I turned my gaze out the window.

"Hmm, I don't know. Maybe it's your nagging, or this bitterness that seems to have consumed you lately. I mean, I made a mistake and I've tried everything to make it right. I've apologized a hundred times, begged your forgiveness, offered to go to counseling, and it's like you take pleasure in my groveling. It's just so exhausting. You wonder why your relationships don't last. Take a look at yourself and ask whether you beat down every man you love when things don't go your way."

I was dumbfounded that he would use something that I'd told him in confidence against me. I'd shared how the only other two real relationships I'd had—with my college boyfriend, Damien, and my last boyfriend, Eddie—had ended because the men had cheated on me.

"So this is my fault?" I spat, my anger rising.

He released a frustrated sigh. "Of course not. I'm a grown man, responsible for my own actions. I made a mistake. No, scratch that, I made a choice. I messed up and tried to do everything to make it right, but you have so much anger inside of you that you won't even entertain trying to fix us, and you damn sure aren't willing to take into account *any* role you might have played in this."

"This isn't on me. This is all you."

"Yeah. All me," he huffed. "Because men love coming home to bitter, angry women every night."

"Oh, but you don't like to address why I was angry."

"Oh, but I do. The whole world knows you wanted a baby and I didn't. You tell every damn reporter in North America," he snapped. "But you fail to tell them that when we talked about that before we got married, you were okay with not having kids."

My chest was heaving as I replied, "I could tell the reporters how you got fixed behind my back to make sure we didn't have kids." Just uttering those words reignited the flame of pain that shot through me whenever I thought about how Jay had secretly gotten a vasectomy. Yes, my husband was right: I'd been okay with not having children before we got married. But I couldn't help it that the motherhood bug bit me. And he wouldn't even entertain the idea. He had a child from a previous relationship who had died in a car accident a year after we were married, so he wasn't the least bit pressed about having another, and that was a constant source of contention for us. I'd only gotten to spend a year with his seven-year-old daughter, but something about spending time with her had awakened my ovaries, and I suddenly wanted a child of my own. And yes, it had left me angry and bitter that he wasn't interested. That anger went to a whole other level when I found out about his vasectomy.

"And I told you that I could get the procedure reversed if we ever changed our minds. But that was a decision we would make together."

"Yeah, like we made the decision about you getting fixed together, huh?" I huffed, then added, "It doesn't even matter now," as I swallowed the lump in my throat. This conversation was moot at this point anyway.

"You're right," Jay said. "But let me let you in on a little secret for your next relationship. And this is real talk. I was wrong to have an affair. But when you beat a man down mercilessly, someone is going to come along and lift him up."

As if on cue, Mary J. Blige began crooning about how she wasn't gonna cry. I pursed my lips and breathed in, then out, through my nostrils. If I was the crying type, my husband's words would have brought me to tears.

I hated that our road had detoured down this treacherous terrain, though. I'd seen it unfolding ahead of us three years ago. It had started eating at me that Jay couldn't, or wouldn't, see that I was passing my prime and desperately wanted a child before it was too late. I didn't want to be changing diapers at forty. But no matter how many times we'd fought over it, he'd been adamant about his position. I had secretly considered tossing my birth control pills, but I knew that emotionally, that wouldn't be a good way to start a family. So I'd given in to his desire to wait. And for what? To find out about the vasectomy.

"It's funny how you place all the blame on me and negate how you wouldn't even discuss what matters most to me," I finally said.

Jay released a heavy sigh as the driver pulled into the reserved parking spot in front of the bookstore. The publicist was waiting outside. She removed the orange cone as the vehicle slid into the space, a huge smile across her face as she waved at us.

Jay stared at the smiling woman. "Can we just go in here and do what we're supposed to do?" he said. "Then, we'll go home and I'll give you your divorce so you can go find that perfectly flawless and faithful man."

"Of course," I replied, with a faux-cheesy grin. "Let's put on our happy faces. Forget the real problems, and go greet our fans. That's what we do, right? That's the whole reason for all of this. To put on a show and make sure the fans are happy."

"What does that even mean?" he asked, exasperated.

I let out a long sigh to match his exasperation. "Nothing, Jay. I'm tired. Can we just do this and get it over with?"

"Fine," he huffed, stepping out of the car. I took a deep breath to pull myself together.

The line for the book signing was already out the door and snaking around the corner. Jay waved to the crowd as he walked around to open the passenger side of the Escalade. I knew the last thing he felt like doing was helping me out, but again, it was all part of the act.

The driver opened the SUV door and I eased a stiletto

out and took Jay's hand as he assisted me; then we both waved to the crowd.

"We love the Lovejoys!" someone screamed.

"We love you back," Jay replied, as he placed his hand against the small of my back and helped me up the walkway.

My smile faded and I struggled not to cut my eyes at him. Of course he'd respond; the woman who yelled had gigantic silicone breasts and bleached-blond hair.

"Can you at least try to hide your attitude?" he whispered through a tight smile.

"Please don't talk to me," I replied, keeping my own forced smile intact.

"Hello, hello," the publicist, Lori, said, greeting us as we walked up. She was a petite, perky woman who was the epitome of professionalism. And her tireless efforts were part of the reason Jay and I had become household names. "As you can see, we have a terrific crowd. Everyone is just so excited about this new book. You guys really have a home run with this one." She held up a copy of our new book, *Real Talk*. Of course she'd be excited about it. The book had been out eight weeks and had been on the *New York Times* bestseller list for every one of those weeks. Our last book three years ago hadn't even made the Amazon bestseller list. But then again, that was before the syndicated radio show, before we discovered the formula to help couples heal their tattered relationships.

Before Oprah.

Oprah had done a special on OWN on black love and featured us. It had aired just over a year ago and the next thing we knew, our lives had changed drastically. We were already a big success with a loyal black following, but Oprah gave us universal exposure and catapulted us into a whole other stratosphere. We'd built on Oprah's magic touch because we were good at what we did—getting couples to right what was wrong in their relationships. So I couldn't figure out why in the world we couldn't work out our own problems.

"These are all the people who bought the VIP package for the retreat," Lori said. "Which, by the way, is completely sold out," she said as she guided us around to a back door.

Jay and I made our way inside the room and over to our table, and for once, I was grateful that this was a straight book signing and not a discussion. Jay's words had hurt me to my core and it was going to be hard enough to smile in each of these people's faces.

Jay and I took our seats and immediately began signing books as Lori kept the line moving. She was great at keeping talking to a minimum.

I was shocked at the number of people here for the VIP signing. Our team had been dumbfounded when we'd learned registration had reached twelve hundred people for the retreat in the first three days. Then, a week later, the Family First Foundation had come on board to sponsor the event, cutting the cost of the retreat in half for any couple wanting to attend. When that announcement hit, the applications started pouring in. We'd had to find another venue because we had initially only planned for about seven hundred; now, more than three thousand people were attending. That was the only reason I'd agreed to move forward with this. I didn't want to disappoint all of these people.

A leggy, brown-haired beauty stopped in front of our table. I couldn't help but marvel at her dang-near perfect body. She looked like she had just stepped off the pages of a fashion magazine. "Hi, can you sign my book?" she asked.

Jay kept stealing glances at the woman. He had an expression I couldn't make out and I was all prepared to give him a *No, you didn't* look, but my anxiety was eased when the woman stepped right past Jay and in front of me.

"Please make it out to Vonda," she told me. "I really admire you. You're such a strong woman. I'm in a relationship myself, but sometimes I get so frustrated with him. So I just applaud how you hold it all together."

If you only knew, I wanted to say.

"Well, frustrations are only natural," I said as I opened the book up to the title page. "But if he treats you right and you love him, you hang in there." I scribbled my name and my standard "Best Wishes" message.

"Oh, I love him, from the bottom of my heart," Vonda said with a smile. "But sometimes I just don't know if he really loves me."

"Well, saying and doing are two different things," I said, handing her the book. "If he loves you, he'll show you with his actions, not just his words."

"You know, you have a point. I can see why you're the best at what you do. That's what I need to tell him. He needs to stop talking about how much he loves me and show me," she declared.

"I'm sorry, we have to keep the line moving," Lori said, gently tapping Vonda's shoulder.

Vonda flashed a picturesque smile as she squeezed the book to her chest. "Thank you so much, Dr. Shannon. You just don't know how much I need this book. And it's obvious that you know the secret to happiness. After I read this, I hope that I'll know it too."

She dropped the book into her bag, not bothering to get Jay's signature before strutting away.

five

This hotel suite was the stuff architecture magazines were made of. The open concept with floor-to-ceiling windows gave us a panoramic view of the island. There were two private balconies, one of which overlooked a heated lap pool.

I made my way into the bathroom, where I removed my clothes and stepped into the shower. As the steaming water from the imported double shower head sprayed my back, I reflected on my relationship.

The way that we were now hurt my heart something fierce. When we first started dating, after the charity auction, I had been a psychiatrist with a thriving practice, a book deal, and family money. Since Jay had lost most of his money over the years, I had been the breadwinner, and had no problem doing so, because Jay worked hard. And now his income rivaled mine.

We'd had a whirlwind romance for a little over a year and a half before Jay popped the question. An elaborate proposal on a Bravo television special had been followed by a beautiful wedding at Trunk Bay Beach on Saint John, in the Virgin Islands—which was why the idea of returning here for the retreat tugged at my heart. I had no desire to go back to the place where I had said "I do" after my husband had made it clear that "he didn't."

For the first two years of our marriage, everything was wonderful. Jay was loving and attentive, and showered me with affection. But somehow, somewhere along the line, my desire to be a mother had overtaken my desire to be a wife.

I just wished Jay could get that. Or that I could get over my resentment. I had done my research. He was right that the vasectomy could be reversed, but not until he decided he wanted it. So even if I could get over him having the vasectomy behind my back in the first place, the fact that he still didn't want kids was causing me immeasurable pain.

I sighed as I turned off the steaming hot water and stepped out of the shower. As I glanced at my reflection in the bathroom, the words that I often said to my patients popped into my head: *Anger benefits no one.* I could never forget what Jay had done, but maybe I could forgive him and move past this anger, because it only seemed to be suffocating me. I'd started having constant headaches, and I was sure it was because I was in a perpetual state of anger.

"Don't be afraid to make the first move. Go talk to him so you can heal," I said, staring at my reflection. That was what I'd told a listener recently, so why was it so hard for me to take my own advice? I knew the answer. Jay and I argued. We didn't talk. And we dang sure didn't listen.

I dried off; then, just as I was reaching for my flannel pajama pants and tank top, I changed my mind and instead opted for a long silk tiger-print gown. I couldn't remember the last time that I'd worn it and didn't even know why I'd brought it. Before I'd discovered the affair, Jay and I had sex once every few weeks, but it had definitely lost the spark that it used to have.

Maybe him seeing me in this would remind him of what he'd tossed aside. Maybe it could help me move past the anger if I could see that he still felt something for me, even if nothing ever came of it.

I slipped the gown on, pinned up my curly brown hair, and sprayed on Donna Karan's Cashmere Mist perfume. It used to drive Jay wild. I thought about stepping into a sexy thong but decided wearing nothing was better. I didn't know why. I didn't want to be intimate with Jay. I just needed to know if he was still attracted to me.

We were sharing the penthouse suite, only he was in the smaller connecting bedroom.

I made my way out into the living area and saw Jay sitting, staring at the television. He looked deep in thought.

He glanced up when he saw me enter and a glimmer of excitement passed through his eyes. But just as quickly as it had come, it was gone.

"I was, um, just wondering, well, I just wanted to say . . . things don't have to be ugly between us." I sighed. "We've both said some pretty foul things and we're mature enough not to end like that."

His eyes roamed up and down my body. "You . . . you look beautiful."

"Thank you," I said, running my hands along the silky fabric. I fought to keep the smile inside from coming out. "I just decided I don't wear this enough."

He nodded as anticipation filled his eyes. He licked his lips and I couldn't help but notice the rising bulge in his pants.

"Jay," I said, but before I could finish my sentence, he stood and pulled me to him, kissing me like he was trying to touch my soul. I was rigid at first, but within seconds, my body relaxed and I returned his passion.

I didn't want to kiss this man, this cheater.

I didn't want my body to respond to his touch.

And I damn sure didn't want to enjoy the feeling that was running through my body.

But in that moment, what my mind wanted didn't matter.

Jay took my hand and led me toward my bedroom. He removed one strap of my gown as he kissed my neck. He eased the negligee completely off as he took my breast in his mouth. He used his fingers to massage my back and all anger and bitterness dissipated and I felt the overwhelming need to lose myself in him.

"I . . . I missed this," he moaned as he pulled my naked body to his.

My mouth couldn't find his fast enough, but once it did, it was as if I couldn't get enough.

I tore away his clothes as he pushed me against the dresser, and within seconds, I lost myself in the pleasure that was his body. His steel-tight chest was hard, as was the part I most craved. My fingers explored him as if I was trying to discover new places. But it was all familiar. All wonderful. All that I needed.

Jay was the best when it came to foreplay. He always wanted to please me. But today, no preamble was necessary. He eased out of his boxers as he continued to caress my body with his tongue. My veins thrummed in anticipation. When we united, our joy was instant.

But it wasn't enough.

Rising from the dresser, Jay carried my 150-pound frame as if I were light as air. Without disconnecting, he laid me on the bed and we sought new pleasure.

Right now, all I could think about was the bliss that was overtaking my body. Ecstasy blanketed me, filling me with sensations that made me pray that we could stay right in this place forever.

I moaned.

He cried out.

Together, we created a chorus that rivaled any award-winning music.

When it was over, I snuggled close to Jay's chest and immediately felt him tense up again. I looked up to see him once again deep in thought.

"A penny for your thoughts," I said through my bliss.

He gently pushed me off him, sat up, and flipped on the lamp next to the nightstand. "I'm sorry," he began. His words were heavy and a mist covered his eyes.

I sat straight up, as a sickening feeling started building in my stomach. "Sorry for what?"

He swung his legs over the side of the bed and stood. "For this. It shouldn't have happened."

"What are you talking about?" I asked, taking in his beautiful naked body. "I think it was long overdue. We're still married and both have needs."

He stepped into his underwear as he shook his head. "No, it shouldn't have happened."

I pulled the down comforter up to my chest but didn't say a word.

He ran his hands over his close-cropped hair, sighed heavily, then said, "You made it clear that you want a divorce. We're here to get through this week, collect our money, and go our separate ways. This"—he motioned between us—"is only going to complicate things."

It felt like someone had taken a sledgehammer and hit me in the stomach. I had followed my heart when my head knew better, and now I was paying the price.

"Is it her?" I managed to say, my voice barely above a whisper. "You feel bad about sleeping with me because of her?"

He bit his bottom lip, as I had learned long ago that he did when something pained him.

When he didn't reply, I felt like I wanted to throw up. This was just as painful as the moment I found out about the affair.

"It's not about her. . . . She's irrelevant. It's just . . . I'm sorry," he said.

I struggled to find my words. Finally I inhaled, then exhaled my next words. "Look, it was just sex. It meant nothing. Thank you. Please turn the light off on your way out." I lay down and pulled the covers up over me so he couldn't see my tears as he left.

six

The previous night had been the longest, hardest night of my life. I had finally cried myself to sleep about 5 a.m. I didn't know how I was going to make it through this first session today. I didn't want Jay to think that his declaration had crippled me, so I had to put on my game face.

"Good morning," Nicole said as I walked into the green-room at the convention center.

"Good morning," I mumbled. I didn't bother removing my oversized Privé sunglasses.

"Ooooh, somebody hasn't had their java this morning," Nicole joked.

I dropped my Gucci bag in the swivel chair in the corner and headed over to the coffee station. Not that Folgers Black Silk coffee was going to help me this morning, but I wanted to feel the warmth of the liquid anyway.

Nicole ignored me and continued mindlessly chirping away.

". . . so we will tape most of the workshops today. The producer from Netflix needs all the footage for the documentary."

I was just about to say something when the door to the studio swung open. Jay walked in, followed by Quincy, our business manager. Jay stopped and his eyes briefly met mine before he looked away.

"Hey, Shannon," Quincy said, walking over and kissing me lightly on the cheek. He did the same to Nicole.

"What's going on, Quincy? You here to do some last-minute legal stuff?" Nicole asked, handing us our day's itinerary.

Quincy looked at Jay and shrugged. "To be perfectly honest, I'm not quite sure why I'm here. Jay called and asked me to be here this morning. And, well, when Jay calls, I come."

I removed my sunglasses and glared at my husband.

"So do you want to tell me why I've been summoned?" Quincy asked. He glanced at his watch like he was on a serious schedule.

"Do I need to leave?" Nicole asked, finally noticing the tension in the room.

"No," I quickly spoke up. Although Quincy was both of our managers, he'd been Jay's friend first. I needed a friend on my side for whatever this was that Jay was about to blindside me with.

"Stay," I added.

"Somebody want to tell me what's going on?" Quincy asked, a wave of anxiety crossing his face. Quincy was about the bottom line, and anything that was affecting our business bottom line was cause for concern. He'd nearly passed out when we'd told him that we were divorcing. And then he'd run down all that we stood to lose financially. I knew he was holding out hope that we would reconcile.

Neither Jay nor I said a word.

"Yeah, Jay, what's going on?" I finally said. "You summoned, so don't act like you're Silent Sam now."

Quincy looked back and forth between the two of us. "Look guys, we have a convention center full of people out there preparing to have the time of their lives. I get it, your relationship can't be healed, but you are amazing at healing others. So for the next five days, that's what you guys will be doing. I thought we were all on the same page with that."

My imagination started running wild. I envisioned Jay telling us all that he was about to marry his mistress. That she was pregnant. Maybe that was why he felt guilty about sleeping with me. Some kind of way, his vasectomy didn't take and his mistress was pregnant. The thought made me physically ill.

"Relax," Jay said. "Quincy is here because I want to make sure we're all aligned."

I felt an instant flash of relief.

"I'm confused," Quincy said. "I thought we worked all of this out before coming to the Virgin Islands."

"We did. But"—his eyes met mine—"I just don't want there to be any confusion. Shannon . . . well, my wife has a vindictive streak, and I just wanted Quincy to remind everyone what's at stake with this conference."

"What the hell is that supposed to mean?" I asked. "Let me guess: you don't want me to tell all your adoring fans that you're leaving me for another woman."

"I am not leaving you for another woman." He turned to Quincy. "See, this is exactly what I'm talking about. I don't want her ruining my reputation with lies."

"Where's the lie? Did you or did you not make love to me last night and then tell me you were in love with someone else?"

"No, I did not." He didn't bother to mask his irritation, but I didn't care. This whole situation had me beyond irritated.

"Oh, I'm sorry, you're just screwing someone else and you were so guilt-ridden over having sex with your still-wife that it ate you up inside," I snapped. "Yet you have the nerve to tell me you don't love her, that she's irrelevant. You're just willing to throw away your marriage for her, so obviously it *is* about her."

"Our marriage isn't ending because of *her*," Jay said. "Our marriage has been over for a while, and you know that."

His declaration stung, but I refused to give him the satisfaction of knowing that.

"No, I didn't know that. I thought we were just having problems like everyone else," I replied.

"Okay, that's enough," Quincy interjected, as the two of us shot daggers at each other.

"Are you okay?" Nicole whispered, squeezing my arm.

I glared at Jay as I fought desperately to keep the tears at bay. "No, but I will be."

"Jay, man, what's going on?" Quincy eased toward Jay.

Jay let out a heavy sigh. "You know what? This is just too much. I don't want to risk what she might do. She can just lead the retreat by herself. We can tell people I have the flu or something. Shoot, she can have the Lovejoy franchise. I'd even be willing to step aside and let her have the radio show."

"Don't do me any favors. He can do the retreat and I can go home," I snapped.

"See, this is why I wanted Quincy here. I just want to make it very clear to her that I will sue her if she further damages my reputation." He turned to Quincy. "Please remind her of the defamation clause in our contract. She's so full of anger."

My mouth fell open in shock. Less than twelve hours ago this man had been making mad, passionate love to me and now he was talking about suing me?

"Oh, this is un-freaking-believable. Let me tell you and Quincy what you can do with that defamation contract."

"Would you two just stop!" Nicole said.

"Yeah," Quincy added. "No one is going anywhere. Or suing anyone. I don't care if you two are fighting like Ike and Tina: you will work this out—at least for now."

We turned our fury on him. He seemed to forget he worked for us. "You have a contract," Quincy explained. The firmness in his voice told us he was serious. "Not only for this radio show, but another book, public appearances . . . and, uh, most important, the more than three thousand people who paid good money to be here." The expression on his face said he was mortified that we would even entertain the idea of bailing on this conference.

"Let me remind both of you." Quincy pulled his briefcase onto the table, popped it open, and began sifting through the papers. He found what he was looking for and slid it across to Jay. "The Family First Foundation has already bought airline tickets, ad time, and paid expenses. They have spent, to date, four hundred sixty thousand dollars."

"What?" Jay and I said in unison. Jay picked up the paper and started reading it over.

"Yes, airline tickets aren't cheap, especially for two hundred couples," Quincy continued. "Then there are hotels and the conference center; when we changed the venue, we incurred additional costs, which they covered, not to mention the labor to set up, and, of course, the advance you guys were paid."

"Well, we'll give our advance back," Jay said.

"I'm not giving back anything," I declared. "We're not canceling because of me. I know how to honor my vows." We had been paid a hefty sum for our services and I had no intention of giving that back. The money was securely tucked away in our joint savings account and even though we would have to split it, I would still get almost one hundred thousand dollars. At this rate, I was going to need every nickel I could get to secure my solo future.

Jay released a groan. "Then I'll just pay back the full advance myself."

Quincy sighed. "Man, are you not hearing me? You're really going to pay back the advance, plus the four hundred sixty grand they've spent on everything, plus whatever they sue you for breach of contract?" He stopped to try to get the emotion out of his voice so that he could reason with us. "There are no ifs, ands, or buts about it. You're contractually bound to go out there and give these people a show," Quincy continued. "Remember, also, you have all the other speakers who have committed. Canceling wouldn't go over well with them. Iyanla turned down another major event. She would definitely sue. And what about the book deal? It's a two-book deal. Not fulfilling the terms of this contract would garner some really bad publicity and your publisher could pull the next book and demand that you pay back that advance. So if you don't give the people what they came here for, you might as well hang up your career. Not to mention the fact that it will bankrupt you."

The room was silent before Jay finally said, "Whatever. I'm good. I came here prepared to do what I had to do, so I'll do it."

"Both of you need to be good," Quincy said, looking at me. "Release the emotions and operate in logic. Suck it up and figure out how to get along, at least through the next week. You do what you gotta do when you get back, but at least for the next five days, the Lovejoys are still one happy couple."

Pain resonated through my body. I trembled as I nodded. "I told you before I came here that I'll do this. So I'll do it. I don't know why Jay felt the need to have you come remind me of that."

I grabbed my purse. "Now, let's go to this VIP meet-and-greet and fake it through the week so my husband can get back home to his mistress."

I slipped my glasses back on and strutted out of the door.

seven

Today had been a rough day. Between the meet-and-greet, opening workshops, and constant press, I was worn out. So much so that I'd hopped in a cab and gone over to Sebastian's on the Beach. It was no Buccaneer, but their cosmos were world-famous and it gave me a respite from Lovejoy fans.

All day long, I'd gone through the motion of existing, because despite my outside demeanor, the quiet reality tore at my insides. My husband no longer loved me. That revelation ripped at my core, and I had to leave before I had a complete breakdown.

I was just about to turn up my third drink when I spotted Nicole standing over me.

"Ummm, how did you know I'd be here?"

Nicole dropped her purse on the bar, then slid onto the seat next to me. "It's my job to know." She smiled. "I hacked your iCloud account and did 'Find my iPhone.'"

"Remind me to change my iCloud password," I said, taking a sip of my drink.

Nicole placed her hand on my arm; her eyes were sympathetic. "How are you, really? I know today was hard."

I shrugged. I didn't really want to talk about it. "I'm fine, I guess."

"Hey, it's just me," Nicole said. "You know you don't have to play the hard role with me."

That was true. The two of us had been through every one of my trifling boyfriends, all my heartbreaks and heartaches, my triumphs and tragedies. Nicole had finally settled down and was happily married to a wonderful man named Emerson, who worshipped the ground she walked on. In fact, every man Nicole had ever dated had put her on a pedestal, and as far as we knew, was completely faithful. She'd never known the heartache of infidelity. Maybe it was her model looks, her gorgeous and fit size 6 shape, and her wonderful personality, or perhaps the fact that she absolutely, positively loved sex—and was open to any- and everything with her man. Whatever the reason, she'd never have to worry about her husband up and leaving. Still, if anyone knew my pain, it was her.

I took a deep breath and finally let a tear fall. "What did I do to deserve this?"

Nicole reached over to hug me. "Nothing, sweetie. This isn't your fault, but I know it's hard."

"You have no idea," I said, lifting my drink to take another sip.

"I'm so sorry you're going through this."

"Me too. I just wish we didn't have to do this stupid retreat," I moaned. "I can't believe I'm going to have to be around him and just pretend everything's fine. It was so difficult today. These past few weeks have been an absolute nightmare. I've never experienced pain like this. I just don't think I can do this."

"Yes, you can," she said. "Just put that facade on for the week and everything will be fine. You're putting on a show, remember? A show for which you're being paid very well. You do your thing; then at the end of the week you collect the rest of your money, get ready to collect half Jay's money, and tell him to go screw himself." She motioned for the waiter to bring her a drink. "Lemon martini, please." She turned back to me. "Has Jay said anything about the other woman?"

"Nope, nothing. In fact, he just keeps trying to play it down and says she has nothing to do with this. He claims he only admitted to the affair because he didn't want to lie to me." I took a gulp of my drink. "He's been lying to me for months, but now all of a sudden he's developed a conscience."

"Maybe he's telling the truth?" Nicole said, nodding her thanks as the bartender set her drink on the bar in front of her.

I swallowed hard. "And maybe I'm going to divorce Jay and marry the Prince of England."

"I don't think they'll let two black girls marry princes."

Nicole was about to say something else when her phone rang. She picked it up and looked at the caller ID. "Oh, shoot, this is the camera crew from the production company we hired here. We've been playing phone tag. Hold on . . . Hello . . . Hey . . . I can barely hear you. Give me a second." She pulled the phone back and looked at it. "The signal is bad in here."

"Go out on the patio," the bartender said as he wiped the bar in front of us. "It's better out there."

Nicole turned to me.

"Girl, go handle your business. Somebody needs to keep stuff together," I said.

She looked apprehensive, then finally said, "Okay, I'm just going to step out to take this call. I'll be right back."

I held up my drink. "And I'll be right here."

As Nicole took her call, I stopped the bartender before he walked away. "Another drink, please."

"A pretty lady like you shouldn't be drinking alone."

I turned to the deep, sexy voice that was coming from behind me. My words took flight and I was left speechless at the sight of the fine specimen standing before me. He had the richest, darkest skin I'd ever seen and a smile that made my woman parts dance.

"Hi, I'm Ivan," he said, extending his hand.

"Ummm, h-hi . . ." I stuttered. Ivan took my hand, squeezing it gently as he shook it.

"Mind if I sit down?" he said, motioning to the empty seat next to me.

I was still thinking about how soft his hands were when he said, "The seat?"

"Actually, umm, well, my friend just stepped outside to take a call." I glanced toward the patio. "She'll be back in a minute."

He slid onto the barstool and flashed that dazzling smile. "Then I guess I have just one minute to convince you why you should have dinner with me."

Maybe it was the cosmos, but his boldness turned me on. Or maybe it was the way that the fabric of his shirt wrapped his chest, just enough to show off his toned body, but not so much that it was too revealing."

I laughed. "You're cute."

He frowned. "I work out six days a week. 'Cute' is never what I'm striving for."

I smiled. "And you're funny."

Ivan glanced down at my left hand. "Ahh, I missed that," he said, noticing my three-carat princess-cut Tiffany ring. "I'm sure the man who bought you that would not like the idea of you going to dinner with another man."

Ivan didn't realize it, but he'd just given me even more reason to entertain him. If Jay could get him something on the side, so could I.

"The ring is just for show now," I said, wiggling my fingers. "The man who put it there didn't care about the vows that went with it, so why should I?"

Ivan smiled just as Nicole approached us. "Ahem," she said, clearing her throat. "Am I interrupting something?" She raised an eyebrow in my direction.

I smiled as Ivan stood and introduced himself. Nicole was obviously mesmerized by his rugged good looks as well.

"Is that real?" she said, touching his biceps.

He flexed his arm. "One hundred percent real. The result of hard work."

Nicole removed her hand like she'd touched a hot stove. "Whew. Well, Mr. Ivan, whatever you're over here talking about, I guess I have to say thanks, because I saw my friend's grin across the room and it's been a minute since I've seen her smile."

I blushed as Ivan softly caressed my hand. His touch sent shivers up my spine.

"And what a beautiful smile it is," he said.

"Umph," Nicole muttered, looking slyly at me. I noticed her expression and shook myself out of the trance Ivan was lulling me into.

"Shannon, I'm gonna have to go back to the convention center. The production crew is having some issues and I'm going to have to take care of them." She glanced back over at Ivan, almost as if she hated to leave. "So, um, are you gonna be okay? I mean, maybe you should come with me."

Ivan and I exchanged glances. I was enjoying our conversation and I could tell he wanted me to stay. And more important, I wanted to stay.

"Nah, I'm good," I said. "I think I'm going to stay and chat with my new friend."

"Are you sure?" Nicole asked. "I mean, you're a little tipsy."

"I'm fine. These drinks aren't strong at all. I'll catch a cab back over when I'm done," I said. When I saw the concerned expression on her face, I added, "I promise I won't leave this facility."

Ivan pointed to the ceiling in the corner of the bar. "And there are security cameras everywhere."

Nicole bit her bottom lip. "Let me see your license," she told Ivan.

I expected him to protest, but he laughed as he pulled out his wallet. "Here you go," he said, handing her his ID.

Nicole took her cell phone, snapped a picture of the ID, and handed it back to Ivan. "A girl can never be too careful."

Ivan shrugged as he took the license and put it back in his wallet.

Nicole was still hesitant but said, "Okay, I'll call you later to make sure you got back safely." She moved closer to me, then whispered, "Are you sure you're okay?"

I flashed a reassuring smile. "I am. I'm sure." And as I gave the gorgeous man in front of me another once-over, I knew I'd never been more sure about anything.

After Nicole left, Ivan and I continued our conversation. It had been so natural to talk to him. I probably overshared—I told him that I was going through a divorce, that I was hurting, that I didn't want be here in the Virgin Islands with Jay. And Ivan had just listened.

"Excuse me, it's last call," the bartender said just as Ivan said something to make me laugh. I was shocked that in the midst of my pain, this man was able to give me some momentary joy.

"Wow, I didn't realize it was so late," I said. "You can close out my tab."

Ivan held up his hand. "Wait, I got it." He slid a credit card across the bar.

"Thank you," I said. "You didn't have to do that."

"I know," he said. "I wanted to."

"I probably have talked you to death," I said. I stood and had to immediately sit back down. "Oooh." I was definitely feeling tipsy.

"You okay?" he asked.

"I'm good," I said, shaking it off. "All the cosmos."

Ivan bit down on his bottom lip. "I enjoyed you."

"I enjoyed you as well. I hate that the night has to end," I said.

He paused, then said, "It doesn't have to."

I felt my insides twitch, like they were trying to answer before my head did. Ivan sensed my hesitation because he said, "Your husband is a fool. Any man who would choose another woman over you needs his head examined."

I paused as his words hung in the air. "You staying here?" I found myself saying.

Ivan nodded. "Room five twelve."

Today was amazing. I will be dreaming about you inside me all night. I love you.

The words of my husband's mistress replayed in my head and I found myself saying, "You feel like company?"

eight

Heartbreak could turn you into a damn fool. I had no doubt of that fact as I assessed my current situation. I was really in a hotel room with a stranger. Even worse, I was really in a hotel room with a stranger, about to have sex.

The battle between good and evil was raging inside me.

"You're better than this."

"You're a grown woman. Do you."

"Jay doesn't want you. Get with someone who does."

"What's good for the goose . . ."

I tried to silence the internal debate. Yes, Ivan was sending electromagnetic waves through my body that I hadn't known were possible. But the fact remained that I didn't know this man. Right now, though, my body didn't seem to care.

Common sense banged on my door, then kicked it in.

"Wait," I muttered as Ivan reached behind my back to remove my bra. Things were moving at rapid speed. "I . . . this . . ." I stopped his hands before they could get the clasp loose.

"Shhh," he told me, taking my hand and gently easing it off his. "Let me make you feel like you deserve to feel." He kissed my neck. I moaned, and then he muttered, "But if you really want me to stop, I will."

"I . . . I'm not thinking straight," I managed to say, my words heavy and hoarse.

Ivan paused, then sat up on the bed. My insides screamed for him to keep going.

"Look, I don't want to take advantage of you but you're a beautiful woman. And if your man couldn't see that and appreciate that, you need to allow someone who does appreciate"— he looked at my body and licked his lips—"appreciate all of this."

That made my heart hurt again and I didn't move from the bed. Jay had told me I wasn't meeting his needs, so he'd found someone who did. Why couldn't I do the same?

"If only for one night," he said, "let me take away some of your pain."

A tear trickled down my face as Ivan lifted my shirt and kissed my stomach. He eased me back on the bed and gently lifted my skirt.

The inner battle continued. "Wait, umm . . ." I moaned. But then my body told me to shut the hell up as his tongue ran along the string of my thong.

"Wait, I'm so sorry. I'm . . . so sorry," I cried, squirming away from him. "I . . . I . . ."

He lifted his head from beneath my skirt. "So you want me to stop?"

"No . . . really. I mean, I . . ."

Where the hell were my words?

"It's okay," he said, pulling himself up. "If I could just give you a moment of pleasure, then I'm happy."

"I—I don't normally do stuff like this." I adjusted my skirt as I scooted to the edge of the bed.

"You don't owe me an explanation," Ivan said. He stood, licked his lips, and smiled. "You're a beautiful woman. But I don't want to do anything you're not ready for." He pointed to the wine on the minibar. "Why don't we just open this bottle of wine?" he said. "And talk. It seems to me like you might need that as much as you need anything else."

I managed a smile. "Wine would be good," I said, even though the cosmos had taken their toll. I was willing to try anything that could distract me from the man in front of me.

Ivan grabbed the bottle and two glasses. "You want to talk about him?" he asked. "Your husband, who is foolish enough to cheat on a woman like you? You touched on it a little, but I'm all ears if you want to talk about it some more."

I thought for a moment. I didn't want to talk about Jay anymore, but I found myself saying, "I tried to be a good wife."

"Yeah. Men are screwups," Ivan said. "I don't know if it's genetics or what." He paused and looked around the bar area. "Well, it looks like there's no corkscrew here. Hang tight. I'll run down to the bar to get one."

I simply nodded as he made his way out the door. His words hung in the room. *"Men are screwups."* That was something my mother used to always say about my father.

My parents. I hadn't thought about them in years. Both of them were gone, but they were the reason I'd vowed not to become some weak, whiny woman.

———————

"Come on here," my mom said as we approached the family having dinner at Legal Sea Foods. I remembered the look on my father's face as my mother stomped toward the table where he was eating with a bleached-blond woman and two perfectly poised–looking children.

"Debra, what are you doing?" my father asked in horror as he looked up and saw us.

I quivered next to my mother, who was wearing a blond wig the same color as that woman's hair. Only my mother looked crazy in her wig.

"Hello, Lucas. Enjoying your little family outing?" my mother asked. "I sure would like to know why my baby can't come and enjoy these fancy dinners."

My father didn't even look my way. He glared at my mother. "We've had this discussion," he said, his tone stern. "Do not come here with your drama or messing with my family."

My mother's hands went to her hips and she did that wiggling thing with her neck that I despised. "Oh, but Shannon's not your family, huh?" she asked.

My daddy finally looked over at me, and my twelve-year-old eyes bugged, but I remained silent.

"I take care of my daughter," he said. "I have never missed a payment."

"Shannon doesn't need your money. She needs your time," my mother yelled. "You're over here with this white woman—"

Daddy cut her off. "What you're not going to do is disrespect my wife with this ghetto foolishness."

Unfortunately, this wasn't the first time that I had been in this situation. In fact, this was a common occurrence. For Christmas the previous year, Mama had put me in a Santa dress and sat outside Daddy's house with a sign that said WHY CAN'T YOUR DAUGHTER COME FOR CHRISTMAS? For my seventh birthday, she'd dropped me off at his job—and left.

It felt more and more like we were living in one of those soap operas that Mama loved to watch.

"Please don't make me take out a restraining order," he added.

"I told you that you should've done that a long time ago," the blond woman muttered. I knew that she was my stepmother, but my mother had forbidden me to ever refer to her as such. And since I'd never spent any time with her, it didn't bother me one bit. But this—my mother acting like a crazed woman and my father looking at her in disgust—did bother me. And I'd begged my mother to stop. By now, I was old enough to understand that he wanted nothing to do with us. I'd accepted it and just wished that my mother would too.

"I'll give you something to restrain," my mother said, taking a step toward her.

My father stood and grabbed her arm. "Debra, if you don't . . ."

She snatched her arm away and I saw the tears pooling in the corners of her eyes. "I can't believe you're doing this to me." And just like that, the tough-girl act was gone and Mama did what she *always did—burst into tears.* "Why are you doing this to us, Lucas? We need you too. I need you."

Daddy huffed, rolled his eyes, then hissed, "What part of 'you were a side chick' do you not get?"

This time, Mama's voice was weak as she said, "I'm a good-enough side chick for you to keep running back to." *I looked at my stepmother, who was now clutching her children's hands. I wondered if these were my siblings whom my mother always complained about. I used to always wish I had a brother and sister, but from the scared looks on their faces, I imagined that they'd never be nice to me. One of them—the boy—looked older than me. Maybe fourteen. The girl, sitting poised in a fancy dress, looked to be about eight.*

"Debra, you need to go," *Daddy said.*

"No! You come to my bed over and over, including last month, and you think I'm just supposed to walk away?"

That made Daddy shift his weight from one foot to the other as an uncomfortable expression crossed his face. Daddy didn't visit often, especially now. When he did used to visit, he always brought me gifts and he and Mama would go in the back to talk. They would send me to my room and tell me to turn the TV up. I guessed it was so I couldn't hear their conversation. And every visit ended the same—with Mama in tears, begging for him not to leave.

Daddy's wife, I think her name was Melissa, was trembling and struggling not to cry. "Lucas . . ." *she said.*

Daddy kept his eyes on Mama as he said, "I'm going to ask you to leave before I call the police."

Just as he said that, a man in a suit walked over to them. "Good evening, I'm the manager here. Is everything okay?"

"Mama," I whispered, as I pulled her arm. "Let's just go."

"No," she replied, snatching her arm away from me and jabbing a finger in Daddy's face. "I'm tired of you hurting me. We deserve you just like they do."

"Lucas, this is unacceptable."

Daddy's wife stood up from the table. I didn't know if she was about to leave or try to beat Mama up—though I was sure my mama would've beaten her to a pulp.

"Honey, just let me handle this." Daddy turned to the manager. "Sir, can you please escort this woman out?"

"I don't need to be escorted anywhere!" Mama screamed. "You love me. You say it every time we make love. So why are you doing this to me?"

The outburst made Daddy's wife burst into tears. Mama was already crying, so it was only natural that I would cry, too, especially as two security guards appeared and dragged my mama out of the restaurant as she screamed, "Karma is coming, Lucas! Mark my words, karma is coming!"

———————

That was the day I lost respect for weak women. There were so many more days like that until eventually the visits from my father stopped, and my mother turned to drugs to numb the pain. Crack gave her the comfort Daddy wouldn't. She became a drug addict all because a man didn't want her.

As much as I loved my mother, by the time I was sixteen, I despised her too. Two months before my seventeenth birthday, my mother's boyfriend at the time decided he wanted out. Mama begged him not to go. They got into a fight and he beat her so badly that her brain swelled. Two days later, she was dead.

That day, standing over my mother's lifeless body at the county hospital, I vowed that I would never chase after a man. It's why every relationship I had, the minute the guy messed up, I was out. I firmly believed that saying "Fool me once, shame on you. Fool me twice, shame on me." I didn't believe in second chances. And I wasn't about to change that with Jay. I wasn't foolish enough to believe in karma either. Though it might have appeared to have caught up with my daddy—he died when I was twenty-three—it was from a drunk driver and no sort of payback for wronging me and my mom.

The knock brought me back from those painful memories and I jumped up to open the door.

Ivan stood there with a big smile on his face. "Sorry, forgot my key. Got the bottle opener." He walked into the room and pointed to the balcony. "Now, let's just go sit out there and talk."

Those words were music to my ears.

nine

M R. AND MRS. LOVEJOY.
I took the place card off the table and tossed it
in the trash can. In about eight months (according
to my research, that was how long this whole divorce would
take), I'd never answer to that name again. Quincy was trying desperately to figure out how to salvage our professional
careers. We'd built them on this seemingly perfect marriage
and our ability to dispense advice about healing damaged relationships. Who would want to take advice from a couple
who couldn't fix their own problems?

I imagined that I'd have to open my practice back up. I'd
closed it after Oprah because I simply hadn't been able to
keep up with the demand.

Sure, we'd made good money so far and I probably could
even go a couple of years without having to work. But since I
didn't like worrying about money, I'd probably jump right
back into the fray. As much as I used to love being a practic-

ing therapist, the thought that I'd have to go back to it saddened me because it would mean I'd failed at something, and I didn't do failure.

I ignored the stare of the banquet manager, who was looking at me like she was trying to figure out why I'd thrown the place card away. I just wanted to put on my mask, accept this award, and resume my day.

I'd sat up talking to Ivan until about 3 a.m. Of course, Nicole had called to check on me and hadn't stopped calling until I'd caught a cab back to the hotel.

It was so ironic that the retreat would begin with this— Jay and me receiving the Spirit of Marriage Award from the Family First Foundation. I had wanted to decline the honor, but since the whole award presentation had been part of the organization's sponsorship, Quincy had informed us that we didn't have a choice.

Now, sitting here in the packed ballroom, I wished that I'd told Quincy we paid him to be a fixer, and that I needed him to fix this.

"Readjust the face," Nicole said, leaning in to me.

"What? I'm fine," I whispered, shifting in my seat.

"No, you're really not fine," Nicole replied.

We were sitting at the head table. Nicole, who was to give this glowing speech about the impenetrable love between the two of us, was on one side. Jay was on the other side, smiling like he didn't have a care in the world. His door had been closed when I got in. He hadn't even cared that I wasn't there.

"Seriously, you are facing all of these people. It's obvious something is wrong," Nicole continued.

Something *was* wrong. I was being lauded for my sham of a marriage? Please.

"Maybe you shouldn't stay out partying all night when we have work to do," Jay leaned over and whispered.

I wanted to take my New England clam chowder and throw it in his face. Instead, I just glared at him.

He pulled back in a huff.

Though I didn't reply, I was sure my eyes spoke a thousand words.

"Come on, sweetie. You can do this." Nicole gently squeezed my hand underneath the table.

I took a deep breath and turned back to my friend. "The question is, can *you* do this?" I pointed to the manila folder in front of Nicole. "I mean, get up there and lie about how perfect this marriage is? Can you really deliver that introduction knowing it's all a big lie?"

"I got this, okay?" Nicole patted the folder. "You just get that disgusted expression off your face."

"Fine." I faked a cheesy grin, then motioned for the waiter to bring me another mimosa. Both Nicole and Jay shot me warning looks, but I ignored them as the waiter filled the glass up. It was my third glass and they hadn't even gotten to the main course of brunch, but after the hellish month I'd had, I felt entitled.

Just as the waiter finished pouring my mimosa, I reached for the glass. Nicole put her hand on my arm. "We'd like some coffee—black," she said firmly to the waiter.

"What are you doing?" My voice rose an octave.

Nicole glanced around the room. Most people were enjoying their food and not paying us much attention, but a few people at the head table were looking our way, including the president of the Family First Foundation.

"Umm, I need you to come with me to the restroom to fix the back of my dress," Nicole announced.

I leaned back and looked at Nicole's dress. "There's nothing wrong with your dress."

"Come on," Nicole said, standing up. She took my arm and helped me up.

I stumbled, then adjusted my skirt, giggling. "Dang, I guess I didn't really need that third mimosa."

Jay looked horrified. I was just about to ask him what the hell he was looking at, but Nicole snatched me away before I could get the words out.

"Excuse us, we'll be right back," Nicole told the emcee, who was looking at us in bewilderment.

Nicole opened the folder and used one hand to point to something inside as she kept her other hand gripped firmly around me. "So I need you to approve these last-minute speech changes," she said, loud enough for others on the dais to hear.

We stepped off the stage and Nicole hissed to a different waiter standing by the kitchen door, "Bring a cup of black coffee to the ladies' room right now."

The waiter scurried off and Nicole pulled me through some double doors.

"Why are we in the kitchen?" I asked, still giggling.

Nicole had closed the folder and was now stomping through the kitchen, nearly knocking over waiters as we made our way toward the back.

"Where's the staff restroom?" she demanded.

A petite waitress pointed down a narrow hall. "Right around that corner on the left."

"Dang, it looks like that show *Hell's Kitchen* back here. Where's chef Gordon Ramsay?" I chuckled at my own joke as Nicole grabbed my arm again.

"Nic, where's the fire?" I said as I struggled to keep up.

Nicole pushed me into the ladies' room. "Have you lost your damn mind?" she said as soon as the door closed.

"Hey, you can't talk to me like that. You work for me, remember?"

"Right now, I'm your friend. Not your employee." Nicole jabbed a finger in my face. "And I'm about to tell you about yourself."

"Tell me what?"

Nicole spun me around to face the mirror. "Look at yourself! *Really?* My friend is the consummate lady! She wouldn't be caught dead drunk in public, and she sure as hell wouldn't be drunk at an event where she's being honored!"

I was about to protest and say that while I might have been a tad bit tipsy, I was nowhere near drunk. Then I saw my reflection. Although I never saw my call-in guests, the woman staring back at me in the mirror was the image of those pathetic women I despised. I had just carelessly brushed my hair, so there were stray strands everywhere. While my outfit was nice, a pink floral belted St. John jacket and skirt, my shoes didn't match. I'd been too out of it to even unpack my other bag and pull out the pair that went with that outfit. Even my mascara had started running. How was that possible? Had I been sitting at the head table, crying?

"Seriously, look at you!" Nicole continued. "You stayed out all night drinking. Then you wake up and drink some more. I know you're hurting, but you've got to pull it together."

I lowered my head in shame. "He's just sitting there acting like nothing is wrong. He broke my heart and he's acting like it's no big deal. And I tried to pay him back last night, but I couldn't bring myself to do it," I finally sobbed. It was the first time I'd truly cried since I'd found out about the affair. "Why do I have a conscience about our vows but he doesn't?"

Nicole pulled me to her and hugged me like she was trying to suck up some of the pain. "Trust me, Jay is hurting too. He just knows he has to get through this week."

"He's not hurting." I sniffed as I pulled back. "This is what he wants or he would've never cheated in the first place."

Nicole rubbed my arms. "Maybe once you make it through this, you can talk about that some more. But you've got to keep it together."

I glanced at the mirror again. "Oh, my God. I look pathetic. I can't do this, Nicole," I cried, grabbing some paper towels off the wall and dabbing at my tear-streaked face.

"You can and you will," Nicole said, her voice firm.

There was a light tapping on the door.

"Who is it?" Nicole snapped.

"I . . . I, um, have your coffee," the voice on the other side said.

Nicole shook her head at me as she walked over and got the coffee.

I glanced back at my reflection. Nicole was right. Never in a million years had I thought I'd let any man—even my husband—leave me literally crumbled and doing things out of character. When Eddie had broken it off with me, I'd sworn off men, but I hadn't shed one tear over him. But this was different. This was the man I'd sworn to love till death did us part.

"Drink this." Nicole returned and thrust the coffee cup at me.

I took it without protest and gulped down the hot liquid. I grimaced—I hated black coffee—but Nicole was right: I needed to pull it together. I was a professional, and no matter what I was going through personally, this was not the way to deal with it.

I took small deep breaths as I stood and tried to get my bearings. Nicole pulled out some more paper towels, wet them, then handed them to me. I took them and dabbed away the smeared mascara. Nicole helped me finger-brush my flyaway hair, then stood back and smiled.

"There, much better," she said, before glancing down at my feet. "Except for the shoes. Is that a new fashion trend, purple shoes with pink floral?"

I managed a smile. "I guess we can say it's a trend now."

"Yeah, I think that's one trend I'll pass on." She grabbed my arm. "Now, come on. Let's go put on an Academy Award–

winning performance; then tonight, we can go back to my room, drink virgin drinks, and talk about how men aren't anything but dogs."

"Except for Emerson. You have a good man."

"And we're going to find you a good man. Someone worthy of Shannon Lovejoy."

"Parker. Shannon Parker," I replied, sniffing as I lost my smile. "I'm going back to my maiden name."

"Whatever you want, sweetie. Just drink the rest of this coffee."

I gulped the hot liquid, then smiled in gratitude. I was glad to have someone like Nicole in my corner. Not only as an employee but, more important, as a friend.

ten

Throughout my marriage, I'd been used to women looking at me with envy. But today, this woman sitting in the first row in the auditorium seemed to be transmitting more than envy. Her face was filled with disdain.

She looked extremely familiar, but my mind was so jumbled that I couldn't place her. She caught me staring, then stood, shot me a hateful glare, and marched to the back of the room.

Nicole arranged some papers on the podium. The event was standing room only.

The rest of the awards brunch had gone off without a hitch, thanks to Nicole. I had even managed to smile and act happy as the Family First president raved about how the Lovejoys were "the example of how all marriages should be." I'd wanted to laugh and tell him how wrong he'd been. Instead, I just nodded and accepted the accolades. And I'd kept my attitude at bay. So I definitely deserved to be awarded. I'd been the consummate actress. Viola would have been proud.

I'd even made it through the day's events without crying or cussing Jay out. But the act was exhausting, so I had turned in early. Now I was refreshed and alert this morning.

"Did you see that woman glare at me, then stomp to the back of the room?" I asked once Nicole had returned to her seat next to me. "I've seen her somewhere before but I can't remember where. Maybe I gave her some bad advice." I shrugged, refusing to give the woman the satisfaction of knowing she was getting under my skin.

Nicole laughed. "Or maybe she's mad because she's alone." Nicole motioned around the room to all the couples.

"Hey, Nicole," Jay said, walking up to the stage.

"Good morning, Jay," Nicole coolly replied. She had to remain professional since she was, after all, both of our producer. But as my friend, Nicole made no secret of the fact that a part of her was hot with him for hurting me.

"Good morning, Shannon," Jay said.

I gave him a terse hello, rose, and walked away. I'd gotten up and worked out this morning and we hadn't seen each other before making our way to this first session.

The event was designed to be a Q&A on what men and women wanted. We got things started, then fell into a natural rhythm as we had a candid discussion about what makes a marriage work. The discussion got heated at times as people asked questions and audience members gave unsolicited input. It took everything in my power to keep from interjecting my personal opinions. But when the woman with the attitude who had been glaring at me stood, took the mic from the intern taking questions, and said, "Can we address the topic of why men cheat?" I knew I wouldn't be able to keep my personal feelings at bay.

The question unnerved Jay and his reaction didn't go unnoticed. He probably wondered if I was going to put him on blast. I decided to step in before he could deflect the question.

"I think that's a great topic to discuss," I quickly said. "Anyone in the audience care to chime in first?"

A lady in the front row raised her hand. "The answer to that is easy. Men cheat because they're dogs."

I second that, I wanted to say.

"If you keep calling a man a dog, don't be surprised when he starts acting like one. After all, you spoke it into existence," some man yelled from the back of the room.

"They cheat because of Viagra," someone else shouted.

"I think they cheat because the sluts they cheat with have no moral compass," another woman interjected.

Another woman in the back raised her hand and immediately began talking. "I take offense to that," she said. "I have dated several married men. But it's not like I go looking for them. They find me."

The woman was wearing a low-cut blouse with cleavage that screamed "Look at me!" *Of course men found her*, I thought. She showcased her boobs like they were a GPS system.

"Don't you feel bad about doing that to another woman?" someone asked the woman.

"That's the thing . . . *I'm* not doing anything to anyone," the woman replied with an attitude. "I have no loyalties to some woman I don't know. If a man is going to cheat, he's going to cheat. That's just how it is. I'm not doing the cheating for them. I'm not *making* the men do anything they weren't already going to do."

Several of the men in the room shifted uncomfortably like they really would rather not have been a part of this conversation.

But the man who had spoken up earlier stood up. "Most men don't wake up and decide, 'Hey, I want to cheat.' They're lacking something," he said.

"Oh, miss me with that bogus excuse," some woman from the left side of the room said.

It was time for me to take back control of this situation before they started yelling at one another. My life was enough of a reality show. I didn't want to turn this conference into one.

"People in committed relationships should understand that there's a profound probability that both parties involved will be tempted," I interjected, "usually several times over the course of their relationship. That's a part of life. What they choose to do with that temptation is up to the involved individual."

Jay wouldn't look my way. He probably knew my eyes were boring into him as I waited for him to weigh in.

"Am I supposed to deny myself something I want in order to preserve the false integrity of a marriage between people who aren't satisfying each other?" the man said.

"The bottom line is that the desire to cheat is a part of human behavior," I continued. "But that doesn't give anyone carte blanche to do it." I turned my attention back to the big-chested woman. "I do agree that you're not the one at fault here—you aren't the one who made vows to someone else; therefore, you're not the one to blame for the failure to honor vows. It's the husband who pledges himself to his wife. He's the one who bears the brunt of the responsibility for being unfaithful to his wife."

"So just remember, ladies," the woman replied with a sly smile, "treat your man right, and he probably won't end up with a girl like me."

"No, you should remember that if he cheats with you, he'll cheat *on* you," someone on the other side of the room snapped.

The woman rolled her eyes at that, and Jay quickly stepped in.

"We really don't want this to turn into a bitchfest on infidelity," he said. "We want to focus on resolving the issues that tear us apart. And one of those is communication. Let's talk about ways to properly communicate."

I glared at him. Of course he'd try to change the subject. But the crowd was game, because someone raised their hand and asked about the five love languages.

We spent the next thirty minutes in candid discussions about that and everything from shared responsibilities to rekindling the magic to the conversation that hurt the most for me—falling out of love.

When we wrapped up and dismissed the participants, Jay quickly began gathering his things.

"We need to get going," he said to me. "We have to meet with the people from the foundation."

I wondered why he was rushing. That meeting wasn't for another thirty minutes. It was obvious anything that shone a negative light on him made him uncomfortable.

"In a minute," I said, turning to talk to a woman who had walked up to have me sign a copy of our book.

I opened the book but kept my eyes on Jay, because the woman who had been glaring at me at the start of the program had walked up to Jay and was standing directly in front of him with her arms crossed.

"Can I talk to you?" she asked.

I stopped in the middle of signing my autograph. At first, I was just glancing out of the corner of my eye. But now I stopped writing altogether. The woman standing in front of me also turned and was watching Jay and the woman, as were several other people in the front of the room.

"I'm a little busy," Jay said, feigning a smile. "I have to get to another meeting."

"Well, we can talk in private," the woman said, motioning around the room, "or we can talk right here, in front of everyone."

Nicole's eyes were glued to Jay and the woman as well. My best friend was poised and ready to take off her producer's hat and go into full best-friend-got-your-back mode.

"Excuse me for a moment, please," Jay finally said to a couple who were waiting to talk to him. He motioned toward a side door that looked like it led to a storage room; then he and the woman headed in that direction. I stood frozen until Nicole shot me a *What the hell are you waiting for?* look.

"Excuse me as well," I said, handing the book back to the woman in front of me. I quickly headed toward the door through which Jay and the woman had gone. I had just reached for the doorknob when I heard Jay say, "What the hell are you doing here?"

I tugged at the door and was angered when I saw it was locked. I tapped on it, even though I wanted nothing more than to kick it off its hinges.

"Jay, it's me, open the door." I heard some mumbling, but the door didn't open. This time, I pounded. "Jay, I swear to God, if you don't open this door, I am about to act a straight fool and you know I'll do it."

A minute passed, then he eased the door open. Defeat blanketed his face. The woman stood there with her arms still crossed, attitude on full display.

I stepped inside the small room, which was stacked from the floor to the ceiling with toiletries and cleaning supplies. An assortment of brooms and mops lined the wall.

"What's going on?" I asked, looking back and forth between the two of them. "Who is this?" I asked, but I already knew. This was the reason my marriage was over.

"Yeah, Jay, tell her what's going on." The woman was defiant. Entitled, even. "Tell her who I am."

My jaw was tight as I looked at her. "How about you tell me who *you* are?" I said.

The woman pursed her lips in defiance but didn't bother to answer.

"Shannon, let me handle this," Jay said. "Please?"

I held up my hand and whipped my head toward my husband. "I'm not talking to you." I turned back to the woman, who slowly unfolded her arms, her hands going to her hips. Jay having an affair was one thing; bringing that woman to this conference was grounds for justifiable homicide.

"If you must know, I'm Vonda Howard," the woman said.

I suddenly remembered where I'd seen the woman. At the book signing the other day—the woman who hadn't wanted Jay to sign her book.

I kept my glare on her as I said through gritted teeth, "Jay, you'd better tell me what's going on before I turn this place upside down."

Jay sighed in resignation.

"You'd better tell her, because I'm tired of this. All these empty promises," Vonda said. Her voice had started quivering now. "I'm fed up with your games. With your lies. And you told me she backed out of the conference."

"Backed out?" I asked incredulously, staring at the woman. "It's the *Lovejoy* conference. Led by both of the Lovejoys. Me back out? What kind of sense does that make?"

"Well, I didn't think my man would lie to me," she said with a smirk. "But I guess I was wrong."

"Vonda!" Jay said.

My man? I felt like someone had taken a bat and hit a home run into my stomach. "Excuse me? What did you just say?" I had heard her loud and clear. I just couldn't believe what I heard.

"My. Man," Vonda repeated.

"Are you talking about my *husband*?" I said, trying to keep my voice steady, as I was sure no one had left the auditorium.

"Your soon-to-be *ex*-husband," Vonda corrected.

"I knew you were low down but this is unbelievable even for you," I said, turning to face Jay. "You not only cheat, but then you have the audacity to bring your side piece to our event?" It was taking everything in my power to keep that South Side of Chicago I'd been reared in at bay.

"No," he protested. "You have to believe that I would never do that."

"Whatever," Vonda said. "You know—"

"Shut the hell up, Vonda, with your stupid, delusional ass," Jay snapped.

She rolled her eyes but shut up. I was in shock. Jay didn't talk to women like that. And what kind of woman would even let him talk to her like that?

"Shannon, please, let me explain." Jay stepped closer to me and I stepped back.

"You are such a liar," I said. I was trembling in fury.

"And don't think you're going to get half our money," Vonda said before Jay could respond. "You need to just lick your wounds and go on your merry way."

My focus immediately shifted back to Vonda. This woman was certifiably crazy. "*Our* money?" I took a step toward her again. So much for appearances. I was about to unleash my rage and beat this woman down in the broom closet. "Bi—"

Jay jumped in front of me to stop me. "Shannon, no, this isn't the time or the place. I'm going to need you to calm down. Please don't let her get you out of character."

That made Vonda's eyes grow wide. "Why are you worried about her, Jay? Huh? What about me? How do you think *I* feel?" she cried. And not just in tone. She had real tears trickling down her face. I couldn't believe this whole scenario. In that moment, I saw my mother pleading and crying and disgust filled my stomach.

Vonda continued. "I'm sitting out there watching you two play lovey-dovey. You told me that your marriage was over, that it's been over."

"Vonda, please just shut the hell up," Jay said, exasperated. He clenched his fists and I swear if I didn't know better, I would think my husband was going to punch this woman.

Vonda crossed her arms defiantly. "All I know is I told you, I'm not going to be the other woman for long, and I'm not. I guess you thought I was playing. I gave up a lot for you, and I'm not going to let you treat me any old kind of way."

I took a deep breath. I was going to take my soon-to-be ex's advice and stay calm. Jay wasn't worth it. "Whatever, Jay. You and this bitch can go to hell."

"I'm a bitch with your man." Vonda chuckled half-heartedly. Her whole demeanor had changed just that fast. "How 'bout that?"

I stared at her with pity. "And you say that like it's a good thing."

"Oh, it is. I know how to keep a man."

I laughed—a deep guttural, pain-filled laugh. Part of me wanted to snatch this woman's long, golden brown hair out of her head. The other part just said, *Let it go*. I would not sully my reputation, my career—over my husband's side piece.

"Sweetheart, he's all yours," I said as I turned to walk out the door. I had finally come to the realization that it was time to let my marriage go, and if Vonda Howard wanted my husband so bad that she would travel halfway across an ocean for him, then she could very well have him!

I ignored Jay calling my name as I headed in the opposite direction of the auditorium.

eleven

was still fuming. I'd been unable to attend any more workshops or sessions yesterday because I couldn't bear to face the people who had to be curious about what was going on with the Lovejoys and that "mysterious woman," as Nicole had referred to her.

But I was scheduled to conduct the first session of today alone, so I couldn't skip it. Besides, I'd decided I wasn't going to let Jay and his mistress make me hide out in my room. I was going to do my job and get through this week; then my husband and that tramp could go live happily ever after.

I didn't know where Jay was, and I didn't care. I'd disappeared after the broom closet fiasco, taking a cab into the city, telling only Nicole where I was going. I'd spent the day sightseeing and losing myself in the solitude of the island's beauty. I'd wished I had Ivan's number, because there would've been no guilt this time.

I'd heard Jay come into the suite last night, shortly after I did. He'd knocked and asked if we could talk, but I'd refused to answer him.

This morning, I'd heard Jay moving about the suite. He'd most likely gotten up and gone to breakfast. Then again, he could've gone to see his mistress. Probably the only reason he didn't spend the night with her was because he didn't want people at the retreat talking.

I pressed the down button to summon the elevator, then stepped on when the doors opened. There were several people inside it, two I recognized from yesterday's session. They flashed sympathetic smiles as I stepped on. I could only imagine the rumors that were swirling around and this was exactly what I didn't want—someone's pity.

"Good morning, everyone," I said, flashing the best smile I could muster.

"Morning," they chorused.

"Dr. Shannon, it's such a pleasure to finally meet you," said a pretty, plump woman to one side of me. She was impeccably dressed, and her blond hair was pulled back into a tight bun. "I'm Jessica Emberly, the wife of the Family First Foundation president."

"Oh, so nice to meet you," I said as the elevator doors closed. I was supposed to have met Jessica this morning at the breakfast. "How was your flight in?"

"Fine. I arrived late last night. My apologies that I wasn't here for the beginning of the retreat, but our daughter opened for the Boston Symphony," Jessica said.

"That is wonderful," I replied. It was no secret that the Emberlys were an all-American family, with a perfect marriage, perfect family, perfect careers. But then again, everyone thought Jay and I had the same thing.

"We missed you this morning," Jessica said.

"Yes, I wasn't feeling well. I guess the traveling wore me out," I lied.

"I know that feeling." Jessica laughed.

The elevator continued down, stopping on a few floors. When the doors opened on the sixteenth floor, I thought I would pass out.

Vonda was standing in the hallway, waiting to go down. She looked like she was going to a runway show. Her hair was on point and her emerald-green silk wrap dress clung to her perfect body. Vonda's smile widened when she noticed me.

"You getting on?" some man in the back asked.

Vonda giggled. "Of course," she said, stepping into the elevator.

I considered getting off, but it would've been so obvious, especially since the two women from yesterday were already looking like they were expecting something to happen.

"How is everyone on this beautiful, glorious morning?" Vonda asked, positioning herself in the corner of the elevator.

"Just fine," a couple of people replied.

"Well, aren't you a chipper little thing," Jessica said.

"Love will do that to you," Vonda replied, as I willed the elevator to move faster.

"Oh, is your husband here?" Jessica asked.

Vonda shook her head. "He's not my husband—yet. He's my boyfriend. And yes, he's here."

"That is just so wonderful," Jessica replied, giddy with excitement. "I love to see young couples in love. That's why I was adamant that my husband get behind this retreat."

"Oh, my boyfriend and I so need this retreat," Vonda said, poking out her bottom lip. "We have a major obstacle keeping us from true happiness, and I'm hoping that by the end of this retreat, we will have worked through it."

"Oh no, I hate to hear that," Jessica said.

Is this damn elevator stopping on every floor? I wanted to scream as the doors opened yet again. There wasn't even any more room. I pounded the close button.

Jessica turned to me. "Maybe Dr. Shannon and her husband can give you a private counseling session," she said. "I'm a big proponent of premarital counseling."

"Oh, I'd love that," Vonda said, clapping her hands together. "Dr. Shannon, do you think you could meet with me and my honey privately so you can help us get rid of our obstacle?" She smiled at me, taunting me with her eyes.

It took everything in my power not to lose it right there in the elevator. "Well, my schedule is pretty full," I said, my voice cold. I didn't even bother trying to fake a smile.

I almost jumped for joy when the doors opened on the first floor. I was the first one off, but Jessica wouldn't let me get far. "Mrs. Lovejoy, hold on a minute."

I stopped, my back to everyone. I inhaled deeply, then turned around.

"Yes?"

"I know you're busy, but I told my husband that one-on-one sessions were imperative"—she smiled in Vonda's direction—"for this very reason. And since we're firm believers in young love, let's try to help these young lovers work it out."

This was just too much. I was about to tell Jessica that it would be a cold day in hell before I ever had a private anything with this tramp, but Vonda spoke up before I could say anything.

"It's okay. I know Dr. Shannon stays busy, so much so that she probably seldom has time for anything or anyone," Vonda said. "Maybe we can see if Jay can give me, I mean us, a private session."

"Well, I guess," Jessica replied, disappointed. "As long as you get in." She patted Vonda's arm. "You have such a warm spirit; I want to see you and your sweetheart make it."

"Oh, I do too," Vonda said. "You have no idea just how much I want that."

"Excuse me, I really must get going," I said. I had to get out of there before I lost it, because right now, the only thing I could think of was how much I wanted to choke the life out of Vonda Howard.

twelve

had known about Vonda Howard for less than thirty-six hours, and already I hated her more than anyone else in the world. It wasn't just the simple fact that she'd had an affair with Jay; it was the way she sashayed around the resort, blatantly antagonizing me. She had been at the last two sessions, and although she'd kept quiet, she sat glaring at me like a crazed stalker. Now she'd even followed us to this reception and was putting on a show, laughing, talking to people, and stealing occasional glances at me. It was almost like she knew I wouldn't retaliate because of all that was at stake and she was intent on torturing me.

Well, Miss Thang definitely didn't know Shannon Parker Lovejoy. Because the space I was in right now, I was ready to risk it all just for the chance to snatch her hair from its roots.

Quincy must have sensed I was on the edge, because he stepped in front of me, blocking the straight-line view I had of Vonda.

"You are better than this," he whispered, trying to get me to make eye contact with him. We were in a meet-and-greet reception at another one of the resort hotels and Vonda was walking around like she owned the place. Quincy feigned a smile. "Plus, there's a reporter from *People* magazine here to interview you and Jay," he added.

"Move, Quincy," I said, not taking my eyes off Vonda, who had walked over to where Jay was talking to a group and inserted herself into their conversation. Jay had immediately walked away. I should've followed, but I wasn't about to give Vonda the satisfaction.

Quincy put a hand on my arm to try to settle me down. "She's just trying to get to you."

Well, it's working, I wanted to say. Instead, I turned my glare on Quincy. "How long have you known?" I asked.

"Don't do this," he pleaded, gently cupping my elbow.

I snatched my arm away. "How long have you known, Quincy?" I repeated. "I know Jay's your boy and all, but how long have the two of you been laughing behind my back about this?"

"No one ever laughed behind your back." Quincy released a long sigh. "And this whole thing is not like that at all," he added apologetically. "Jay really does love you. This whole affair thing, he was not thinking straight. He felt like you two had just grown apart."

"That's bull, Quincy, and you know it."

"Can we just work through all of this when we get back home?" Quincy asked.

"I had planned on doing that, until his mistress showed up. But I don't know how much more of this harassment I can reasonably be expected to take," I said.

Just then, Nicole and Jay walked up with a tall brunette in a business suit. Jay's eyes all but begged me to cooperate. I glanced over at Vonda, who was now standing in a corner by herself, sipping a glass of wine, her eyes glued to our every move.

"Hi, Dr. Lovejoy," the woman said, extending her hand. "I'm Ava Cole, a freelancer with *People* magazine. I've been assigned to cover the conference. As you know, Family First is a huge organization and the fact that they've gotten behind you so wholeheartedly is testament to their belief in you. Mind if I ask a few questions?"

I kept my smile pasted on as the reporter pulled out her digital recorder and started firing questions. Jay had the audacity to step next to me and put his hand against the small of my back. I tensed up at his touch. Vonda was still standing in the background, glaring at us.

"I don't want you to lose it in front of the reporter," Nicole leaned over and whispered as Jay was answering a question. I glared right back at Vonda. Obviously, I won the stare-down, because she turned and walked away.

After the interview, Jay and I had begun talking to some more people when we noticed the reporter talking to Vonda. She had her tape recorder positioned right in front of Vonda's mouth and was doing an interview.

"I don't think so," I mumbled, stomping toward them.

"Shannon, no," Jay said, stopping me.

I gritted my teeth. We'd been pretty busy all day long, so I was sure Jay hadn't had a chance to talk with Vonda yet, but he needed to do something. "It's one thing for me to stay here in this sham we got going, but I will not be disrespected because you wanted your ho at our event!" I hissed.

"Shannon, I promise you, she is doing this all on her own. I would never bring her here," Jay protested.

For some reason, I believed him. Jay didn't like confrontation and he had to have known having the two of us together could lead to World War III. But that didn't change the way I felt.

"Get this under control, Jay," I said. "This is your mess—now clean it up."

"I told you, it's not like that. She's crazy. I can't control her." I had never seen my husband so flustered.

"Well, you'd better try to put that dog on a leash, because trust, you don't want me to do it. I will blow up everything we worked for before I keep letting her try and torture me." I spun around, took a deep breath, forced a smile, then walked over to Vonda and the reporter.

"Ms. Cole, I didn't know you were interviewing conference attendees," I said.

Ava grinned, like she was thrilled that her story was coming together. "Yes, we like to hear from the people as well. And trust me, they have nothing but rave reviews."

Vonda scooted over next to Jay, who had followed me over, probably to make sure nothing got out of hand. She draped her arm through his.

"I was just telling this lovely reporter how you helped me find true love," Vonda cooed.

"And I just think it's so wonderful that you were able to help someone who was so jaded about the idea of love discover how important it really is," Ava said.

I felt hot tears burning the backs of my eyes. I was so about to lose it.

"So," Ava said, raising an eyebrow like she knew there was more to the story, "tell me exactly what it was Jay said to make you want to give love another chance."

Vonda released a blissful sigh. "He's just such an insightful man. He knows how to get at the core of issues. He helps you find that inner thing that makes you special, and he makes you feel worthy of love."

"Unh-unh," I said, stepping forward to cut this sham short. "Ava, right?"

Ava nodded.

"This is a bunch of—"

"Bunch of information to digest," Nicole said, swooping in out of nowhere. "But we really don't want to bother our attendees anymore. Thank you so much for the interview, but we have to get ready for the evening's event." She pulled Jay away. Vonda, however, wasn't going to release him.

"Oh, I see you really did have an impact on her," Ava chuckled. "She doesn't even want to let you go."

A half-nervous, half-disbelieving laugh escaped Jay's throat.

"Oh, she's about to be impacted, all right," I mumbled.

"Excuse me?" Ava said.

"Nothing," I muttered, backing down. "I was just saying that we really do need to get going."

"Okay, I think I have enough," Ava said, flipping off her recorder.

"Hey, before they go, why don't you get our picture to go with your story," Vonda suggested. She was grinning like this idea was something that had just popped into her head and not something that she had been plotting since this event started. "You know, focus on one of the women Jay helped to find love again."

"What a wonderful idea," Ava said, motioning for her photographer to come over.

"Oh, I don't think so," I said.

"It's okay," Jay whispered to me.

"No, it's not," I retorted.

Ava's eyebrow rose, causing me to add, "It's just that we really need to get going." I flashed a faux apologetic smile.

"Oh, it'll only take a minute," Vonda said, tossing her hair over her shoulder and snuggling close to Jay.

"Well, since the Lovejoys are a team, we'll both get in the picture," I said.

Vonda looked like she definitely hadn't been expecting that as she squeezed right in the middle of us. I didn't even try to force a smile as the photographer snapped away.

"Okay, that's it, they really have to get going," Nicole repeated.

"Thank you both so much. You have no idea what it means to be able to share in this beautiful experience," Vonda said.

She smiled at me and then leaned in and lightly kissed me on the cheek. The only thing that kept me from attacking her was that the photographer still had his camera poised to start snapping. Visions of myself, crazed and enraged, on the cover of the *National Enquirer* caused me to just turn and walk away.

My cooperation in this sham was about to go out the window, and I really had no idea how much more I was expected to endure.

thirteen

This woman was determined to make me lose it. First the *People* magazine interview, now this?

"Are you stalking us?" I said. I didn't care that there was a small group of women standing around chatting. We were off-site at a private VIP dinner. Jay and I had just arrived and were being greeted by throngs of people, when out of nowhere, Vonda popped up. We'd had private counseling sessions most of the day (and I'd felt like a hypocrite during each one). I had been relieved to escape the Vonda drama, but lo and behold, here I was again.

"Maybe Jay wanted me to meet him here," Vonda said, smirking.

"Vonda, you know I didn't ask you here," Jay protested. "I haven't even talked to you, so stop playing these games."

I was surprised to hear that. I'd thought for sure they'd hooked up when I stormed out of the reception last night. Yes, he'd come back to the room about an hour after I'd left, but I had just assumed that he'd spent some time with Vonda. Granted, because he stayed locked up in his room and I was in mine, I was never able to ask him.

Vonda flashed a seductive smile. "Oh, Jay, it seems you're the one who likes to play games—with women's hearts. You're lucky I love you, though."

He thrust his hands up in exasperation. "What is wrong with you? What are you talking about? And the bigger question: why are you even here?"

"You know you want me here," she purred. "You're always talking about how I make you feel like a man." She glared at me. "Unlike wifey, who likes to emasculate you."

"Vonda," Jay said slowly, "you need to leave before I have security throw you out."

"I told you—doing something like that could get very ugly." She wagged her finger like she was chastising a child.

"At this point, I don't care, because this is bordering on harassment."

Bordering? I wanted to say. But if I opened my mouth, it wouldn't be pretty, so I just kept taking slow, deep breaths.

"Fine, I'll go." She stuck her bottom lip out playfully, then glanced around at all the people staring at us. "I know you're working right now anyway. I'm in room 1623. I expect to see you there." She glanced at her watch. "What time do you think you'll make it by?"

This woman has truly lost her mind, I thought. I'd had enough.

I stepped toward Vonda, so close that I was assaulted by her peppermint breath. I jabbed a finger in her face. "You know what? I am really sick and tired of you, and I'm about half a second from choking the life out of you."

"Go right ahead," Vonda said with defiance. "Then I can sue you and get your money *and* your man."

"Vonda, enough!" Jay snapped.

"No. I'm not going to let her scare me."

The two of us stood in a face-off; several people had started staring.

Jay lowered his voice as he took Vonda's elbow and led her over to a corner. It was almost as if he knew he'd have better luck getting through to her in private.

Of course, I followed them.

"Why are you doing this?" Jay pleaded. "This is my livelihood you're messing with."

Vonda's bottom lip trembled as she spoke. She finally was shedding some of her cockiness. "You don't get to play games with me, Jay Lovejoy. I served my purpose, so now you think you can just toss me to the side? It doesn't work like that. You don't get to just play with me, then walk away." She was getting loud and emotional, and the growing crowd was all ears.

"Vonda, please lower your voice," Jay hissed.

"Why?" she said even louder, pointing to me. Jay turned around, noticing me behind him. "Because we don't want the world to know the Lovejoys' perfect marriage is a lie?"

Two security guards walked up in the middle of her rant. "Ma'am, you need to leave. This is a private event."

I stepped on the side of the men. "You might want to listen to them before you get hurt."

"You don't scare me," Vonda said, wagging her finger in my face. She was like a crazed woman now. "Like you could really hurt someone. Please."

"Try me and I'll show you just what I'm capable of," I said through gritted teeth. The two of us once again stood face-to-face, Vonda looking smug, and me, full of fiery anger.

"Come on, Shannon. Let's go," Nicole said, easing up behind me, seemingly out of nowhere. "You are above this."

"Yeah," Vonda chirped, "Miss Prim and Proper has to keep up appearances. That's why your husband strayed in the first place. Didn't your mama tell you a man wants a lady in the streets and a freak in the sheets?"

I heard several people around us gasp, but my focus wasn't on the crowd. I couldn't help it: I lunged at Vonda, but one of the security guards grabbed me and pulled me back before I could make contact.

"Uggh, I'm gonna kill her. Let me go!" I yelled, trying to jerk free. "She's messing with the wrong one!"

"Stop it!" Nicole yelled. "Let's go." She didn't give me time to respond as she yanked my arm and dragged me out the room and into the bathroom.

Nicole locked the door as I furiously paced back and forth. My rage felt like hot lava. "Can you believe the nerve of this trick? Just one good punch to the throat. That's all I need."

"Calm down, Shannon. You're not punching anyone."

I balked at my friend. "Calm down? This woman is making my life a living hell and you want me to be calm?" I screamed.

"Don't give her that power over you. You keep letting her push your buttons. It's obvious she's crazy. Jay already told you he's not leaving you for her, and he said he didn't invite her here."

"And you believe that?"

Nicole nodded. "After seeing that psychopath? Yes. So don't give her the satisfaction of pushing you off the deep end."

"Whatever, Nicole, I'm not trying to hear this." I stopped pacing and took a deep breath. "But I tell you what I *am* doing. Not this. I'm done. I'm going home." I leaned into the mirror to check my reflection and make sure that I'd pulled myself together and didn't look the hot mess that I felt.

"The formal banquet is tomorrow. You cannot leave."

"Watch me." I threw the bathroom door open and literally bumped into Jay, who must've been standing right outside, waiting for us to come out.

"Shannon, can we talk, please?" he asked.

I glared at him, willing the tears to stay back. "If you know what's good for you, you will get the hell out of my face."

Jay's shoulders drooped in defeat. "It . . . it's not what it seems. I'm not with her. I'm not in love with her. I don't want to be with her. I didn't invite her here. I don't want to be within a hundred-mile radius of her."

"Really, Jay? Because it seems like you've empowered the skank enough to feel like she can come to our private event and torment and harass me. You gave her that power." I jabbed my husband in the chest with my forefinger.

Jay ran his hands over his head, his face filled with exasperation and regret. "I messed up. She is bona fide crazy. I am so sorry."

"You know what you can do with your apology?" I tried to push him out of the way. I had to get out of this bathroom before I suffocated. "Now, move."

Jay refused to budge. "Just hear me out. I don't want you leaving like this."

I threw my hands up in resignation. "I wasn't enough for you. You wanted someone who wasn't angry and bitter and who fed your monumental ego, you got it. Now go live happily ever after with her psycho ass, because I'm done. Screw endorsements. Screw contracts and book deals. Just tell everybody to sue me, because I. Am. Done. I'm going home." I turned to my friend. "Nicole, get me out of here before I end up doing something I regret."

I burst out of the bathroom and ignored the rest of the people staring at me as I pushed through the crowd and out the door and headed out to the driver. My only goal was to pack my bags and get the hell out of the Virgin Islands ASAP.

fourteen

My wardrobe was feeling my fury. The meticulous care that I usually took with my designer clothes was out the window. I had dared a tear to fall as I crammed my Chanel into my carry-on, threw my Tory Burch into my tote, and stuffed my St. John into my suitcase.

Although it had been too late to get a flight out tonight, I'd be on the 6 a.m. flight out in the morning. I couldn't get off this island fast enough.

"Unlike wifey, who likes to emasculate you."

Ugh. Why were Vonda's words haunting me?

I took a deep breath. Maybe because they were true. And if Vonda knew that, it was only because Jay had shared it with her.

I slid down onto the bed as my mind raced back to the first time I'd become cognizant of that nasty habit.

The dinner party had gone off without a hitch, and I paid the caterer as I walked him to the door. I surveyed the few people left in our living room: Nicole and Emerson, and April, another one of our friends from college and her date, Devin.

"So what do you think?" Emerson asked just as I walked back in.

He'd just pitched some type of investment idea to us. Jay had been listening intently and I could tell by the way that his mind was churning that he was seriously considering it.

"You know, I think you're onto something," Jay said. "But I'll take a look at the proposal, and we'll let you know."

I refilled my glass of wine. I probably should've stopped three glasses ago because I wasn't much of a drinker, but Jay and I had been arguing earlier about something trivial and I just needed to relax. I sipped my wine as I stood against the bar. "He means, 'I'll let you know because those "Touch My Insides" checks have long since dried up,'" I giggled.

The room grew silent.

"What?" I asked, glancing over at the shocked look on Jay's face. "Sweetie, everyone knows, the things you used to do, you don't do anymore." I laughed at my reference to another one of his late nineties hits. "But luckily you have me to hold it down." I reached over to playfully squeeze his chin.

Jay jerked out of my reach. "Are you kidding me?" he asked.

All eyes remained on me. "What?" I repeated, looking from Jay to our friends, who were all staring at me in amazement. I shook my head because my vision was getting a little blurry.

Jay didn't say another word as he stood, marched into the kitchen, and grabbed his keys off the counter.

"Where are you going?" I asked, as he stomped toward the front door.

"You're drunk, and I'm leaving before I say something I regret."

"I'm not drunk," I replied. "I may be tipsy, but all of us are drinking."

"And you seem to be the only one who isn't handling it well," April said, taking my glass from my hand.

"What is wrong with you?" I called out after Jay.

Jay still didn't reply as he slammed the door on his way out.

I turned back to my friends. "Did I do something wrong?"

"Wow at the fact that you really have to ask," Emerson said.

"That was messed up, Shannon," Nicole said.

I shrugged as I fell back onto the sofa. "Did I lie, though?" When we'd first married, Jay had still had a nice savings account, but he'd made one bad investment after another, and for the past year, I'd been the breadwinner of the family.

"You don't need to say everything that you think," Nicole said.

"Yeah, especially when it means putting your man on Front Street like that," Emerson added.

The look of disgust on Emerson's face surprised me.

"You just straight emasculated that man," Devin added.

I wanted to tell him to shut up because he didn't even know us like that.

"Really?" I said. "Get out of here, I didn't emasculate anyone. Plus, I was kidding with him." I rubbed my temple. My head was now pounding.

"Were you?" Nicole asked.

I rolled my eyes and shrugged. "I mean, it's the truth, but what's the big deal?"

"You emasculated him," Emerson repeated as he stood.

Devin stood as well. His look of disgust matched Emerson's. "We just got through discussing why men go and cheat with the clerk at the corner store," he said, referring to their heated conversation at dinner. "Because a man needs to feel like a man. And what you just did . . ." He shook his head as he motioned April to his side.

"Oh no, you're not going to blame a man's infidelity on the woman," I retorted.

Devin stared at me. "I'm not. Men who cheat do it because they want to. No doubt about that. But while you're making a man feel like a peasant, someone is around the corner ready to make him feel like a king."

Emerson moved toward the door as he added, "That dude goes out into the world every day as a black man. And then to have to come home and have his wife cut off his balls . . ." He let his sentence trail off and shook his head like he couldn't even stomach being in the same room as me.

"Nicole, I'm ready to go," he said, as if I couldn't tell based on the fact that he was already by the door.

Emerson and I had always gotten along well, but the way he was acting now, you'd never have known it. Emerson shook his head again. "I'm a little shocked. You're a therapist, so you should know better."

"Guys, let up off her," Nicole said, looking at me with pity in her eyes. "She had a little too much to drink and is acting out of character."

I attempted to stand up to follow them, but I felt a bit dizzy, so I just sat there. "You guys are being overly dramatic," I said. "I was just messing with Jay. But I'm not even trippin' on his feelings.

Why would Jay go cheat when he has all of this?" I motioned around our elaborate penthouse that overlooked the city. "I've given him a good life."

"I guess he had nothing to do with that?" Devin asked.

"And that's just it," Emerson added, motioning around the house. "All of this is for you women. Men don't care about a big house full of designer stuff. What we want is to feel appreciated, respected. Do some men cheat just because they're dogs? Yeah. And do some cheat because they want to feel like a king? Yes."

"Oh, so it's my job to stroke his ego?" I folded my arms across my chest.

"Yeah, it is. Just like it's his job to stroke yours," Emerson said.

"April, your friend is a piece of work," Devin interjected.

I wanted to tell April to get her boyfriend of the month out of my face. Instead I just turned to Devin and said, "First of all, you don't know anything about me to judge me."

He didn't give me time to get to my "secondly," because he just said, "And after tonight, I see I have no interest in knowing you at all."

The sound of my cell phone chirping brought me back to the present. I fumbled for the phone and found it sitting at the foot of the bed.

The chirp was a text from Nicole: *Don't want you to be caught off guard. Check your Instagram page.*

I clicked the link that Nicole had sent and my Instagram page popped open. I took a deep breath to contain the bile building inside my throat.

Every time I thought things couldn't get any worse, they evolved to catastrophic levels. And this was an impending EF5 tornado.

This tramp had no limits. Had she really just tagged me in an Instagram post? And was her profile picture really a shot of her sitting on Jay's lap?

I opened the picture that she'd just posted—a view of the island with two wineglasses positioned prominently in the photo.

Loving the view from my room in Saint Thomas with the love of my life. The real woman always wins. The post had been made twelve minutes ago.

I clicked on Vonda's name and went to her Instagram page. Her pictures were public for everyone to see. Every other photo was of her and Jay. At the beach, at dinner, at what looked like a family event. They looked like a happy couple in love.

I couldn't believe Jay would not only disrespect me like this, but that he'd be so careless as to let her take all these pictures. Or maybe he'd been callous. Maybe he simply didn't care about my feelings. Maybe all that nonsense he'd told me about her doing all of this on her own had been a lie.

Either way, this now gave me grounds for leaving when all these people tried to sue me. Who could blame me for bailing after seeing this? Yes, come tomorrow morning, I would be gone and wouldn't have to deal with Vonda Howard anymore. And as quickly as I could cut Jay from my life, I wouldn't be dealing with him either.

I tossed my phone and tried to sleep, but the rage wouldn't let me rest. This woman had tormented me for the past few days and I was just going to slither away in defeat. The more I lay there thinking about that, thinking about all that Jay and I were losing, about my broken heart, the angrier I became.

After another thirty minutes of seething, I decided I wouldn't be slithering away. Oh, I was still leaving, but not before putting this woman in her place. Less than three hours ago, Jay had been trying to convince me that "it wasn't what it seemed." Now he was laid up with Vonda in her hotel room? No, I couldn't leave without telling both of them a few things about themselves as well.

I stomped out into the suite to see if Jay was back. Of course he wasn't. His door was wide open and the bedroom empty. I grabbed my cell phone and punched Jay's number in. I cursed when it went straight to voice mail. I was determined not to leave this island until I unleashed my wrath on both of them. Then I was going to tell Jay he didn't even need to bother coming home. I would pack his crap up and leave it on the curb.

I was just about to come up with some lie to get Vonda's room number from the front desk, when I remembered Vonda's words. *"I'm in room 1623. I expect to see you there."*

I ignored the little voice in my head telling me *Don't do it.* I was glad that I'd gotten rid of Nicole, because I was on a mission. I was about to get ghetto-girl fabulous and hurt somebody. I didn't care if Vonda sued me; I didn't care if the tabloids got ahold of it. Right now, the only thing that would give me any type of satisfaction was beating the hell out of my husband and his tramp.

I grabbed my card key and stomped toward the elevator. It seemed like an eternity before the button chimed and the doors swung open. I stepped in and quickly punched the button to the sixteenth floor. The doors took their time closing, as if some outside force was trying to give me time to change my mind.

"I don't think so," I mumbled, pounding the button again. There would be no mind-changing today.

I stepped off the elevator on the sixteenth floor. I sprinted down the hall to Vonda's room and was just about to bang on the door when it swung open. Jay stood there, his eyes going wide with shock when he saw me.

"Why doesn't it surprise me that you would be here?" I said, my face masked with fury.

"I, no, it . . . it's not wh-what it looks like," he stammered, trying to close the door and step into the hallway. He looked absolutely panicked about being busted. Probably because there was no talking his way out of this.

"Oh, it's exactly what it looks like, and I'm about to tell you and this wench where you can go." I pushed past him and into the room with a force I hadn't known I had.

"Shannon, wait!" he yelled, trying to grab my arm. Nothing he could say could stop me from unleashing my wrath on that tramp.

I ignored him as I stomped into the room. The smell of sweet lavender assaulted my nose. I guessed Vonda had been setting the mood for a romantic rendezvous with Jay.

The string of curse words was on the tip of my tongue, but then . . . I stopped and all the air in my lungs seeped out. I blinked. Blinked again. Then tried to process the sight in front of me.

Surely this wasn't real. Surely this wasn't Vonda's body sprawled out on the floor. The way her leg was bent slightly to the side, the way her head was positioned, the way her eyes stared at the ceiling . . . I knew. This was no doubt her and she was no doubt dead.

She was wearing the same clothes from earlier, but now a long silk scarf was tied tightly around her neck, a look of horror frozen on her face.

"Oh, my God." I gasped as I backed into the wall. I looked up at Jay, who had followed me into the room. He looked frantic and disheveled. "Wh-what did you do? Is—is she dead?"

"Let's go. Let's get out of here." Jay's voice was panicked as he walked over and pulled me away.

I was frozen in place and couldn't move, despite the fact that Jay was jerking me toward the door. Finally, I stumbled out behind him. We had just stepped into the hall when I popped back to my senses.

"Let go of me," I said, pressing myself up against the wall in the hallway, away from him. "What did you do?" I repeated. Jay, the lover, the charismatic heartthrob. The man I'd loved for years—was a murderer?

"I didn't do anything," Jay protested.

"You killed her? Oh, my God." I glanced back toward the

room and a rush of panic swept over me. "You killed her," I repeated in stunned disbelief.

Jay grabbed me and shook me. "Stop it. Calm down." He forced me to look him in the eye. "Look at me. You know me, Shannon. You know I didn't kill anyone."

I shook my head and wriggled from his grasp. Would he kill me too?

"No, no, I don't know you anymore. I don't know what you're capable of," I said slowly. In fact, I was finding more and more each day that I didn't know my husband at all.

"Yes, you do. You know me." His voice was thick with desperation. "I may be a cheater, and even a liar, but you know I'm not a killer."

"Is she . . . is she dead?" I sniffed, trying to make sense of all this.

Jay released a heavy sigh and looked around the hallway. "I think so."

Suddenly, images of Jay strangling me until the last breath escaped my body, then leaving me for dead, since I had all but witnessed his crime, filled my mind and fear consumed me again. Before I knew it, I took off running down the hall. I had just barreled through the door and into the stairwell when Jay grabbed me and pushed me up against the wall.

I was terrified as I struggled to break free. "I won't say anything, Jay. Just let me go. Please, just let me go," I begged, after it became obvious his grip was too tight for me to get away.

"What?" he said, looking confused before it dawned on him what I was saying. He released me from his grip and stepped back. "Shannon, come on," he pleaded. "I'm not going to hurt you. You know I didn't hurt Vonda."

I stared at him, everything inside me wanting to believe him. But I had also believed that he loved me and wouldn't cheat on me, and look how that had turned out.

"Shannon, you've got to believe me," Jay cried. "I found her like that. I just got there right before you did, and I found her on the floor like that."

I backed up again, shaking my head as if I could fling the image of Vonda's lifeless body away. "I don't have to believe anything—only what my eyes tell me." I glanced toward the room and swallowed the lump in my throat. "And they tell me your mistress is dead."

He exhaled in frustration, then looked at me and said, "How do I know you didn't kill her, then come back here to make sure she was dead?"

"What?" I said.

His eyes were pleading. "That's my point. I know better. Just like you should know better."

I paused. I was furious with my husband. But I couldn't believe he was a killer.

"Well, if you didn't kill her, then who did?" I asked.

"I don't know." He sighed and began pacing in front of me in the stairwell. "I swear, the door was cracked and I walked in. I saw her lying there, checked her pulse, saw that she wasn't breathing, then I was about to get the hell out of there. That's when I bumped into you."

He sounded so convincing. Still, I eyed him skeptically.

"Babe, you've got to believe me."

"I don't have to believe anything," I shot back, suddenly remembering the events of the past few days. "You left me for her, remember?"

"I keep telling you, you wanted the divorce, not me. I didn't want to be with Vonda." I had never seen Jay so . . . desperate for me to believe him. He looked me straight in the eyes and his voice was sincere as he continued. "Yes, I had an affair with her. It was stupid and wrong, but I did. I may have even led her on, because it was the easy way out—or so I thought. But I swear I didn't invite her here. I had no idea she was coming. And I came here tonight to give her a piece of my mind about the stunt she pulled today and I found her like that."

Everything inside me told me that Jay was telling the truth, but still, I didn't know what to believe. What he said, or what she said.

No. I shook my head. No matter what we had been through, my heart knew the truth: Jay was a lover, not a killer. He barely raised his voice to me, no matter how much I pushed his buttons. He couldn't be capable of murder.

"We need to call the police, then," I finally said.

"And say what?" he asked. "We'll be thrust into the middle of a murder investigation. The whole sordid affair will come to light."

Suddenly, any sympathy I'd had for him dissipated. "So that's what you're worried about? People knowing the truth—that you cheated on me? I'm sure they've already figured it out, the way she's been traipsing around the island."

He groaned and rubbed his head. He was definitely rattled as he paced the small corridor. "No, Shannon. I mean, of course that wouldn't be good for our careers. Everything that we worked for will be destroyed. But that's not what I'm focused on. We just don't need this, and remember, several people heard you threaten to kill Vonda earlier as well. This could get ugly for both of us."

"Me?" I stared at him in disbelief. "You know I didn't do this."

"I know that, and you can probably eventually convince the police of that. But are you ready to be questioned? Are you ready to be carted off to this backwoods police department while they figure it all out?"

"I didn't have anything to do with this," I repeated, my voice quivering.

"Where were you at the time of the murder?" he asked.

My glare was piercing. "I was in my room, packing to get out of here."

"Who was with you?"

"I was by myself."

"That's my point," he said. He was pleading with me. "Yes, you can tell the police about that, and they may believe you. But what if they don't? They'll interview everyone who was at the party. What if they say you were so mad about the fight that you followed her back here and killed her? The publicity of our arrest could bring a lot of attention to the police department, and what if they want to make some kind of example? Are you really willing to take that chance?"

Tears started flowing as the reality of what he was saying set in. "So what are we supposed to do, just walk away? Act like we were never here?"

"We don't know for sure that she's dead," he said. Even as the words left his mouth, I could tell he didn't believe them. "Maybe she's just unconscious."

"Didn't you say you checked for a pulse?"

"Yes, but I'm not a doctor. I don't know what I'm doing."

"Which is even more reason to call for help."

I took a step toward my husband. I had to reason with him. I couldn't stand Vonda, but we couldn't just run off and leave her.

"Jay, think about this, what if someone saw you?"

"Nobody saw me."

"You don't know that. And what if your fingerprints are in the room? Because I'm sure you've been there." I couldn't help getting a dig in.

He released an exasperated sigh and I immediately regretted the comment. Now wasn't the time for cutting remarks. We were in a serious situation.

"No, I haven't been in her room," he protested. "I told you she's crazy. This was my first visit. And I didn't touch anything."

"Did you push the door open?"

"Yes."

"Then you touched something," I said, as it suddenly dawned on me that I'd pushed the door as well. "So we'll call for help. We don't have any other choice," I added.

Jay released a dejected moan. "You're right. We can't just leave her."

"Come on." I had just turned and was about to head out of the stairwell when I bumped right into a man who could've played linebacker for an NFL team. He was about six-foot-four, with broad shoulders, eyebrows that met at the top of his nose, and long, cinnamon-colored dreadlocks. He shot us a menacing glare.

"Excuse me," I said, trying to go around him. The man stepped to the side with me to keep me from passing. "I said, excuse me," I repeated. The man just glared at me, refusing to move. Before I could say anything else, the man growled as he eyeballed Jay. "You're Jay Lovejoy," he said. I couldn't tell if it was a question or a statement.

"Who wants to know?" Jay asked, eyeing the man right back. He was trying to sound cocky, but I could feel the fear.

A tight smile spread across the man's face. It made me uneasy.

"Yeah, I'll let you guys handle whatever this is," I said, motioning between the two of them as I tried to step around him again.

"Nah, I think you need to stay with my man here," the man coolly said, moving over to block my path again.

"I don't think so," I said, trying to go around him. "I have a plane to catch in a few hours." Now, more than ever, I couldn't wait to get off this island.

Aggravated, the man pushed me so hard I fell back against the wall. "Little lady, you're hardheaded. I said, you're not going anywhere."

"Hey! Get your hands off my wife!" Jay jumped toward

the man, who quickly pulled out a black pistol and pointed it right at Jay's forehead.

"Are we feeling heroic today?" he asked with a sneer.

Jay froze, and I instinctively stepped behind him. Were we actually about to be robbed on top of everything else?

"Man, we don't want any problems," Jay said, holding up his hands.

"Yeah, neither do I. I've had my killing quota for the day and I'd really like not to have to add another body to my list."

At the mention of bodies, I stiffened.

"Wh-what do you want with us?" Jay stammered. The way he tensed up, I could tell he was thinking the same thing I was—that this man had murdered Vonda and we were next.

"I want you"—he waved the gun at Jay, then leaned over and pointed it at me as I cowered behind Jay—"and you to come with me."

"Why?" Jay asked.

"You sure got a lot of questions," the man said. "Because I said so, that's why. Now, let's move. And no funny stuff or you'll be reunited with your girlfriend real fast."

I felt my stomach sink. This could not be happening. My husband's mistress had been murdered and now we were being kidnapped by the person who'd probably done it.

"Listen, mister," I began, stepping from behind Jay, "it's like you said. This is about Jay"—I glanced sideways at him—"and his girlfriend. This has nothing to do with me." I felt a twinge of guilt over throwing Jay to the wolves, but I quickly shook off the feeling. If he'd gotten into some kind of trouble with that trick he was messing with, then he'd have to deal with it on his own. I wasn't down for dying for anyone. And I definitely wasn't dying for my philandering husband.

"See, that's where you're wrong," the goon said. "Number one, I know you're wifey, so like it or not, you're involved and you might have some info as well."

"Info about what?" both Jay and I said at the same time.

"And number two," he continued, ignoring our question, "I don't leave witnesses."

Witnesses? I thought in horror. What did that mean? And if he didn't "leave witnesses," did that mean he was going to kill us whether we went with him or not?

"Let's move!" He nudged my head with the gun. "And don't try to be no hero," he warned both of us. "My trigger finger is jumpy."

Fear engulfed me as I led the way down the stairs. I looked for an escape route, all while trying to contain the rage brewing inside of me. When we got to the second floor, I debated darting off and into the hallway, but I knew the gun was pressed firmly in Jay's back, and as much as I hated him right now, I'd never forgive myself if he got shot because I tried to make a run for it.

We reached an exit door at the bottom of the stairwell. Jay's eyes were apologetic. I looked away. His affair was the reason we were in this boat. So, no, I might not have wanted this thug to shoot my husband, but as soon as I got away, I was going to figure out a way to kill Jay myself.

fifteen

This could not possibly be happening. The dreadlocked man had moved over to me and now had the pistol positioned squarely in the middle of my back. He had once again warned us that if either of us made a move, he would plant a bullet right in the middle of my spine.

"And if it doesn't kill you, it would leave you paralyzed for the rest of your life," he added. "So unless you want that, move your pretty little tail." He pushed me with the gun out into an alley on the side of the hotel. I prayed that one of our fans, a bellhop, anybody would see us. But we'd barely stepped outside when a beat-up Ford Explorer sped toward us. The driver stopped, got out, and looked at his partner with confusion.

"Hey, Will, what's going on?" he asked in a thick West Indian accent.

The thug looked at his partner in disbelief, probably because the driver had just used his name.

The driver looked like he was about to apologize, but Will held up a hand and stopped him. "We got company." Will threw the front door open.

The driver didn't say another word as he ducked back in the vehicle.

"You. In the front seat. Shut up and ride," Will said, pointing the gun at Jay. "Me and the pretty lady are going to sit here in the back." He opened the back door and pushed me inside. This felt like something out of a bad movie. "And let me remind you, any quick movements"—he looked at Jay but raised the gun to my temple, causing me to cower in fear—"and I might just get trigger happy."

"Please," I cried, squinting my eyes as the cold steel touched my skin, "this has nothing to do with me."

"Shut up," Will barked.

"She's right," Jay said, turning around in the front seat. "Just let her go. She doesn't have anything to do with any of this."

Will took the butt of the gun and hit Jay across the back of the head. Jay screamed in agony and held his head, which had immediately started bleeding. I stifled my scream for fear that I would be next.

"I told you to shut up. Let's go," Will snapped to the driver.

"Here." The driver threw an old, dirty towel at Jay. "You're bleeding all over my seat."

Jay grimaced as he placed the towel to his head to stop the flow of blood.

"Where are you taking us?" I asked after a few minutes of riding in silence.

"You talk too much. Now sit over there and shut up before I stop being nice."

I leaned back and pursed my lips, my eyes on the gun now resting in his lap, its barrel pointing directly at me. I didn't want to push him to the point of snapping, but I desperately wanted to know where we were going, what they were planning, and why in the world they thought I knew anything about whatever it was that had led them to commit murder and kidnapping.

Jay kept glancing back at me, desperately trying to make sure I was all right. I wanted to scream at him, ask him what the hell he and his side chick were into and tell him to do something, anything, to get us out of this mess.

After a few more minutes, we pulled into the parking lot of the Red Star Ferry. My heart started to race at the sight of the large vessel sitting in the water, ready to set sail. If we left Saint Thomas, there was no telling what these thugs would do to me and Jay.

"You got your piece?" Will asked the driver.

"You know I do," he replied, patting his hip.

"Good. Your contact is working?"

The driver nodded. "We're all set."

"Then let's roll," Will said, opening the door and dragging me out behind him.

My heart felt like I'd done cardio, run a marathon, *and* danced all night, the way it was beating so fast.

"When we get on the ferry, you go up front with lover boy and I'll stay here with the little lady," he told the driver.

"That way, if either of them makes a move, we can blow the other one away."

Will leaned into me. "Don't even think about screaming," he said, as he wrapped his arm around me like we were two lovers going to enjoy a scenic view of the Caribbean, "or I promise you, you will regret it. Not only will I shoot you"—he paused and motioned toward a little girl in front of us with long, bushy pigtails, playing innocently with a doll—"but I'll plant a bullet in that sweet little thang's head as well."

I quivered in fear. I felt a sliver of hope as I saw a security guard patting down people as they walked onto the ferry. Surely he would see the gun, feel my terror, something. But when we approached the guard, he made eye contact with Will, then stepped aside and let us pass.

As if Will knew I was preparing to scream or take off, he squeezed my arm tighter and pushed the gun farther into my side. We boarded the ferry and I felt my heart drop as the driver led Jay to the other end of the boat. Will and I sat down behind the little girl with the pigtails.

"Please, will you tell me what's going on?" I said once the ferry backed up and was on its way.

"The only thing I'm going to tell you is to shut your trap. And that's the last time I'm going to tell you that."

I quietly sat back and tried desperately to keep from crying while Will whipped out a cell phone and tapped a name on the screen.

"Hey," he said, his voice low, "we're on our way. . . . Yeah, we got him. But we got company. . . . The missus was with him, so she'll be joining us. . . . Cool. We'll be there in a minute."

He hit the screen, dropped the phone in his pocket, then cut his eyes at me as I sat sniffling and struggling not to cry. "Here, put these on," he demanded, giving me a pair of men's sunglasses he'd pulled out of his pocket.

I took the glasses and slid them on. The few people on the ferry were oblivious to me anyway, so my being teary-eyed wouldn't have done anything but make Will mad.

We rode across the water and although it seemed like it took forever, according to my watch, it had actually only been just over two hours. Signs welcomed us to Saint Croix. When we docked, Will led me off the boat, the gun once again positioned at my side to remind me to do as I was told. Jay and the driver were close behind us. I glanced back at Jay. I could tell his mind was racing, probably trying to think of ways to get away. I was now torn as to whether he should try anything, because these guys seemed ruthless.

Another beat-up Explorer, this one dark gray with rusting doors, was waiting, with another driver inside. Will pushed me inside the vehicle, then pushed Jay in next to me. Jay instinctively grabbed my hand. And though my mind wanted to react, my body welcomed his comforting touch and I squeezed his hand back. Will climbed in next to Jay and the first driver climbed into the front seat as we took off.

The driver of this Explorer didn't say a word as he pulled away. He looked like he couldn't be any more than seventeen, and the way Jay was eyeing him, I could tell my husband was assessing whether he could take him out. I squeezed Jay's hand tighter and shook my head. Will would shoot him in the back before he even made contact with the young driver.

We all rode in silence for ten minutes before pulling up to what looked like a run-down abandoned building. This was definitely not the part of the Virgin Islands they feature in the travel brochures.

"Will someone tell us what's going on?" Jay demanded as we were pulled out of the SUV. Of course, no one said anything as they pushed us toward the door.

"This is ridiculous, we don't know anything," Jay protested. "Why are you kidnapping us?"

The men continued to ignore us as we were led inside the building and up several flights of stairs, then thrown into a dingy room with dirt-covered walls and a tattered rug. The stench greeted us at the door. The place looked like some sort of warehouse that hadn't been used in decades. There were weeds coming in through the loose frame around the lone window near the corner. Empty water bottles and other trash were strewn all over the room. An old mattress sat on the floor in one corner, and four metal chairs occupied the middle of the room. The room was void of anything else.

I couldn't help but wonder how many people had died in this room.

Will kept the gun pointed at me as the first driver proceeded to tie Jay to one of the chairs. The younger driver pushed me down and tied me up as well.

"There," Will said after we were both securely bound. He walked over and patted Jay's face. "You might want to get some rest, my man, because it's going to be a long night."

With that, all three men laughed as they walked out the room and left Jay and me squirming in our seats.

sixteen

Every gangster movie I had ever watched flashed through my head and I knew it was just a matter of time before these thugs shot me execution-style in the middle of this dirty, pissy room.

We sat tied to the chairs. Jay hadn't stopped squirming, as though if he moved enough he could loosen the rope. I had given up because the rope was causing burn marks on my arms.

"Would you stop it?" I finally hissed.

"What would you suggest I do? Just wait for them to walk back in here and kill us?" he snapped.

At the mention of dying, my heart sank, the knots in my stomach tightened, and my anger returned.

"What is this about, Jay?" I asked.

"I have no idea, Shannon."

I cut my eyes at him. "I hope it was worth it. I hope it was just that good to you that it was worth both of us dying for," I said.

Jay stopped squirming and stared at me like he wanted to say something, then decided against it and turned his attention back to trying to break free.

After a few more minutes, he fell back in his chair, frustrated. "It's too tight," he mumbled.

I didn't respond as we sat in silence. I envisioned the headlines when our bodies were found. Would Vonda's murder be pinned on us? Was that the legacy we would leave behind? Was this why God had never given us kids? So that we wouldn't leave them parentless after being murdered in a crappy warehouse?

Finally, after what seemed like an eternity, the door swung open. Another guy with a headful of blond dreadlocks tied up in a ponytail walked in, followed by Will and the driver. The young-looking driver was gone. In his place was some mini Hulk who looked like his mama had named him Killer.

"Jay, my man," the dreadlocked guy said, his arms outstretched like he was greeting an old friend.

"Do I know you?" Jay asked.

The man chuckled as he stopped in front of Jay. "No, but you know someone I know, very, very well." He flashed a wicked grin.

"What are you talking about?" Jay asked, trying to shift in his seat.

"Your girlfriend, Vonda."

"Man, what do you want with us?" Jay asked, not bothering to hide his agitation. "Vonda is not my girlfriend."

"Just call me Max," the man said, throwing his leg over a

chair and plopping down in front of us. "Well, as you've probably deduced by now, your girlfriend was dabbling in some things she shouldn't have been dabbling in and she has pissed some very important people off."

"I don't know anything about her past," Jay protested.

"Oh, I'm not talking about Vonda's past," Max said, that stupid smile still on his face. "This is her present. And Vonda is presently in possession—"

"*Was*," Will interrupted matter-of-factly.

Max snapped his fingers and laughed. "That's right. *Was* in possession of a very important belonging that she was holding for a friend of mine. Vonda is . . . gone to glory now, isn't that how you guys say it back in the States?"

"Well, I don't know anything about anything that Vonda was into," Jay said.

Max sighed like he didn't believe Jay; then, out of nowhere, he stood, walked over and punched Jay in the right eye. I screamed as Jay grunted in pain.

"I don't like being played for a fool, my man. So I'll ask you again, where is it?" Max demanded.

Jay squinted with pain, then shook it off. "Hit me as many times as you want and the answer will still be the same," he managed to say. "I don't know what you're talking about."

"And I don't either," I chimed in. "This has nothing to do with me."

"Ah, yes," Max said, walking over and caressing my hair. "You just happened to be in the wrong place at the wrong time, beautiful."

"Then let me go and I promise I won't say a thing," I pleaded.

"You'd leave your devoted husband?" Max said, feigning shock.

I glared at my husband. Whatever was happening right now was the direct result of my husband's philandering. "Well, obviously my husband wasn't too devoted to me. So you guys can work this out among yourselves. I don't need to die because my husband chose to mess around with the wrong woman."

Jay looked at me apologetically. "My wife is right," he said. "She doesn't have anything to do with this. I'm begging you, please, let her go."

Max wagged a finger. "Ah, but I'm afraid I can't do that." He began pacing back and forth across the room. "See, we happen to know that the night Miss Vonda stole from my client, you were the one who picked her up, Mr. Lovejoy. And if you know something, there's a strong possibility that your wife here knows something as well."

"I just found out about their affair a couple of days ago, so I wouldn't know anything," I protested.

"And I have no idea what you're talking about," Jay said, exasperated.

"Mr. Lovejoy, I don't have time for games." Max turned to Will. "What type of car does Mr. Lovejoy drive?"

"A black Range Rover, chrome wheels, clean as a whistle," Will said with admiration.

"Clean as a whistle," Max repeated with a smile. "You picked Vonda up and took her back to her place. So I'm sure she told you what she was doing."

Jay shook his head defiantly. "I promise you, she didn't. I don't have a clue what you're talking about."

"So you deny picking her up from the W Hotel about six weeks ago? I think it was actually the first of the month," he said, stopping and leaning over Jay.

When Jay didn't answer, Max continued. "And you want me to believe that you didn't bother asking what she was doing at the hotel when you picked her up?"

Jay let out a defeated sigh. "She said she had a meeting and I was just picking her up and giving her a ride home because her car was in the shop."

"Ah, but at her place, you got out and went inside. And you stayed until very late at night, roughly three a.m."

I tried kicking him. That was the night I'd cooked dinner and waited all night for him. That dog had lied and said he'd been at the twenty-four-hour Starbucks working on our next book and lost track of time.

"Oh, my bad. The missus must not have known about that." Max laughed. "You two can work out that little lovers' spat later. Right now, we have business to tend to." He resumed pacing, his hands behind his back. "Let me explain my predicament, Mr. Lovejoy. I have been hired to do a job—deliver a product to my client. My men and I have traveled from the mainland trying to track this vixen down. We have incurred tremendous expense and invested quite a bit of our time. So I assure you, I will get what I seek." He turned and glared at us. "I need the jump drive."

"I don't know what you're talking about," Jay slowly repeated, his voice cracking with fear. "I don't know how many other ways I can say that."

Max continued talking as if Jay hadn't said a word. "Just before she . . . um, transitioned to the afterlife, Vonda informed my associate that she had given you the jump drive. And that has to be true, because it's nowhere in her house."

"What is on this jump drive?" Jay asked.

"That information is provided on a need-to-know basis. And you, my friend, don't need to know." Max eyed Jay suspiciously. "Unless, of course, you already know."

"I don't know anything!" Jay yelled again.

"He's telling the truth," I countered. Though I had no idea whether he was telling the truth or not. At this point, I would say anything to get them to let me and Jay go.

Max held up his hand to quiet me. "Ah, but it seems there's a lot about your husband that you don't seem to know. So I don't think you have a clue whether he's telling the truth or not."

"Please, sir, let us go. You can tell your associate Vonda did all of this on her own. We're not involved in this," I pleaded.

Max laughed again. "You just don't know how deeply you're involved in it, thanks to lover boy here."

I glared at Jay again. Right now, I hated him with every ounce of my soul.

"I sense a little hostility here," Max said flippantly, as he pulled up the chair and sat back down. "Let someone else doctor you, Dr. Shannon. Tell Mr. Max what the problem is."

I didn't say anything as my chest heaved up and down out of a combination of fear and anger.

"Talking about it is the first step in getting through it." He gave a terse grin like he really expected me to open up.

"You want to know what the problem is?" I finally said. "I'm stuck in an abandoned building with some maniacs and I have no idea what they're going to do with me. And why? Because my husband was off chasing whores."

"Ooooh." Max chuckled. "Such strong language." He turned to Jay. "Were you chasing whores?"

Jay pursed his lips. It was obvious his frustrations were mounting, but I couldn't have cared less. "I wasn't chasing whores." He looked down in shame. "Vonda was the only one. I made a big mistake." He glanced back up at me. "All we do is fight and I wanted out of that exhausting cycle."

"No, you wanted *in*—in another woman, and you're trying to use our problems to justify your actions," I snapped at him.

"It must suck to be betrayed," Max said pointedly.

"You don't know the half of it." I rolled my eyes.

Max stuck his bottom lip out sympathetically. "How could he do you like this? I don't know much about you, but you seem like you've been a loving wife." I nodded. "And despite your marital problems," Max continued, "you stayed true to your vows, right?"

I hesitated, then slowly said, "I stayed true to myself."

"Ah, ah, ah," Max said, waving his index finger from side to side. "You didn't answer the question."

"What are you talking about?" I asked.

Max smiled as he motioned toward the thug who'd been standing and guarding the door. The Hulk henchman nodded, then opened the door.

"Come on in," he said to whoever was on the other side.

My mouth dropped open at the sight of the man who walked into the room. "Ivan?"

The tall, attractive man I'd met at the bar stopped and smiled. "In the flesh, baby," he said, his voice deep and seductive and instantly transporting me back to that night at the hotel.

I immediately looked from Ivan to Max, then back at Ivan. "What's going on?" I said. "How do you know them? You told me you were an insurance salesman from Miami."

Ivan shrugged. "I lied. Sorry, bae."

"Okay, what is going on?" I asked.

Silence filled the room as Max stifled a chuckle. It was obvious he found the whole scene amusing.

"Yeah, what's going on?" Jay repeated, his eyes darting from me to Ivan and back.

"Ahh, my love," Ivan said, ignoring Jay, walking over to me, taking a strand of my hair and twirling it around his fingers. "I am looking forward to tasting you again."

I heard Jay gasp but I didn't look his way. "Did you set me up?" I asked Ivan.

"Oh, just trying to see how much you knew about Vonda. Got a little distracted by your"—his eyes roamed down to my lap—"your sexiness." He turned to Max. "But I guess that's one of the perks of the job." He chuckled as Max nodded in agreement.

"Who the hell are you?" Jay yelled, squirming violently in his chair.

"How is my little butterfly?" Ivan said, fingering my thigh on the exact spot where my tattooed butterfly was, the exact spot that he'd kissed, and licked, and caressed until I begged for him to stop.

"Shannon, what the hell is going on?" Jay yelled, his chest heaving, his anger palpable.

Max busted out laughing, as did the rest of the crew. They really were getting a kick out of the show.

"Looks like you two have some discussing to do," Max said. "Good thing we're waiting on the call to see what our next move will be. So make yourselves at home. We'll be back shortly. Happy chatting."

With that, all of them left the room.

I would've given anything if I could've gotten up and left with them. The way Jay's eyes bored into me, I knew he was about to lose it. And that made me mad. The audacity of him to be angry about the idea of me being with another man.

"I'm going to ask you again, what is going on?" Jay said, after it became obvious I wasn't going to say anything.

Of course I felt awful about Jay finding out like that, but I decided the best route was to fight fire with fire. "Don't you dare ask me about anything that I've done. You're the cheater, remember?"

"It sounds like we both are," he replied, his voice filled with anger.

"I . . . I was true to my vows . . . until I discovered you weren't."

He looked at me in disbelief. "I can't believe you. You've been playing the victim, acting all holier than thou, judging me for cheating and you cheated yourself?"

"It was a one-night stand! A half a night at that, since we never had sex."

"That's bull."

"We didn't have sex," I repeated.

"He tasted you!" Jay screamed. "That sounds like sex to me. And you met him here on the island and slept with him. What kind of woman are you?" he added with disgust.

"Are you serious?" I said, shocked at his nerve. "You cheated on me, then turned around and brought your mistress to *our* retreat! What do you think that did to me? I had too much to drink."

"Oh, come on now, can't you do better than blaming it on the alcohol?"

I wanted to scream, but I didn't have the energy. I fell back in the seat and said, "I was hurting, so I sought comfort in the arms of another man. There, does that make you feel better?"

Jay shook his head as a mist covered his eyes. "I don't believe this. As much as you were riding me and acting all hurt and betrayed, and you cheated on me too."

"I *was* hurt and betrayed."

"I guess that makes two of us, then."

"Well, now you know how it feels." I paused. "No, I take that back. You don't know how it feels, because I'm not in love with anyone else."

"Neither am I."

"And I didn't have anyone claiming they love me, following me to the Virgin Islands."

"Obviously, your stalker was already here."

That stopped me cold. I'd fallen for whatever game Ivan was playing. I'd been used—the very thing I vowed I'd never be.

Jay and I were quiet again, and this time, our silent pain spoke volumes.

seventeen

Why in the world was my husband's pain bothering me? He'd started this. As I watched him sitting in the chair, his head hung low, a dark circle forming under his eye where Max had hit him, I could tell he was hurting. But I could also tell that the pain inside him was much deeper than anything physical he might be feeling.

"So you actually had sex with someone else?" he finally whispered.

"Again, I told you that I didn't."

"Well, you were intimate with him."

"You saw it for yourself—they set me up."

"Why would they do that?"

"I don't know, but it's obvious it has something to do with this mess here."

"Maybe so, but they didn't put a gun to your head and make you sleep with someone. You did that all on your own," he said, his voice ripe with pain.

I felt a flutter of shame. I couldn't believe I'd fallen so easily for Ivan. But his attentiveness, smooth voice, sexy accent, and impeccable physique had sent my mind reeling. "I just needed someone to comfort me. I just wanted to be wanted," I admitted. "You slept with me, then acted like it disgusted you."

"It wasn't that. I . . . I just didn't want to make things any more complicated than they already were."

"It just felt good to be wanted."

The words looked like they hurt Jay almost as much as the blow to his eye. "I'm sorry," he finally muttered.

I probably should've said, *I am too*, at that point, but I couldn't bring the words to form in my mouth. While I took responsibility for my own actions, Jay had basically pushed me into the arms of another man.

Our conversation was interrupted as Ivan reentered the room. "Hello, princess," he said, strolling over to me.

"Ivan, what kind of game is this?"

He pulled a chair up and sat in front of me. "It's not a game."

I studied him. He'd seemed so genuine. Never in a million years would I have guessed that it was an act. "Is Ivan even your real name?" I asked.

He nodded. "And in case you're wondering, what we shared was very real too."

"Obviously not, since you set me up."

He shrugged nonchalantly. "It was business, not personal."

"But why me?" I asked. I knew this conversation was paining Jay, but thankfully he remained quiet.

Ivan glared back over his shoulder at the door, then turned back to me. "They just wanted to find out what you knew, if you knew anything."

"Well, you know I don't know anything. I talked to you about what I was going through. If I remember, you even asked me if I knew anything about the other woman and I told you I didn't."

He nodded. "I know. I told them I didn't think you knew anything. But the rest of my team doesn't agree."

Jay started rocking back and forth like he was trying to keep himself calm. I ignored him and continued talking to Ivan. "What are they going to do to us?" I asked.

Ivan shrugged. "Your guess is as good as mine, but I imagine it won't be pretty."

I decided to take a chance. "Ivan, you know I don't know anything. I mean, we were just together that one time, but we talked and I was open with you. You know I was telling the truth." I could feel the fury coming from my husband, but that couldn't be my focus right now.

Ivan nodded. "I do believe that you don't know anything. Not so sure about hubby over there."

"He doesn't know anything, so please just let us go," I said. "Please." I hesitated, then added, "We'll pay you. Whatever they're paying you, we'll double it. I give you my word. You know how to find us, so you know that I'm not going to double-cross you."

I had expected him to balk at the idea, but I saw a light go on in his eyes.

"My wife is right," Jay added, seizing on Ivan's hesitation. "Name your price."

"One million," Ivan said, like he was just throwing a number out.

"Done," I said. That was almost all our savings, but it was better than being dead. "Our business manager, Quincy Haynes, will make sure you get the money."

"Don't play with me, because I *will* come find you," Ivan warned. He had a shocked expression, like he hadn't expected us to really offer him money.

"We have no doubt that you will," I said. "So I assure you that you will get your money."

He paused, like he was actually contemplating our offer. "Okay, I'm going to let you go."

"Thank God," I said, relief consuming me.

"Now, I'm going to untie you guys. Max and the other guys ran out for a few minutes. I'm supposed to be gone, too, but I doubled back. They'll probably be gone for about twenty minutes or so," Ivan said. "That's enough time for you to get out of the building. You need to get as far away from the islands as you can. Go back to the States."

"And go where? How are we going to get off Saint Croix?" Jay asked. "And then how are we going to get on the plane in Saint Thomas? I'm sure the cops are looking for us by now. They probably think we had something to do with Vonda's murder. We can't chance the airport."

I hadn't even thought about that. I didn't know how long we'd been here, but it had to have been at least five or six hours. We'd missed the first morning sessions and they had for sure found Vonda's body by now. We probably were the talk of the island.

"You can leave here through that door," Ivan said, standing and pointing to a door at the back of the room. "Right on the other side is a fire escape. Quietly take that down, make your way out to the main road, and have a cab take you to the port to catch a seaplane over to Saint Thomas. Go to the Virgin Airlines baggage counter and ask for a guy named Talib. I'll let him know you're coming. He'll get you on board the flight."

"This isn't some trick, is it? I mean, how do we know we can trust you?" I asked.

"How do I know I can trust you to give me my money? Besides, do you have any other choice?" he replied.

I stared into his eyes and knew that he was my only hope. I said a little prayer that he was on the up-and-up as he began untying me.

"Why are you helping us?" I asked.

"Like I told you, this wasn't personal. I was just doing my job. Business. And if you can offer me a better business deal, I'm rolling with it." He stroked my cheek. "And truth be told, being with you is something I would've done for free. I hope we can one day reconnect and I can finish the job."

"What the—?" Jay kicked violently at Ivan.

"Calm down, Jay," I snapped. His jealousy was about to blow our chance at freedom.

"Yes, calm down, Jay." Ivan smiled, licking his lips seductively as he stared at me. "Your woman just had an itch that was in dire need of scratching and I was happy to oblige. So while you were off taking care of someone else's needs, I was taking care of hers."

I wanted to give Ivan a piece of my mind for playing me, but since right now he was our only hope at freedom, I bit my tongue. "Can you just help us get out of here?"

"Look," he said as he went back to untying the rope around my arms, "I'm going to help you, but honestly, they're just going to find you again. These people don't play."

"But we don't have anything to do with whatever they're after," I protested.

"Then you might want to find out who does. Just get them what they want. These people don't play fair. And unless you want me after you as well, I suggest you call this Quincy dude and tell him I need my money."

"I told you you'll get it," I said.

"Cool. And don't let the sweetness fool you: I can be ruthless when someone screws me over. I'll send info on how to reach me through your switchboard at the radio station." Before Ivan finished untying the rope, he leaned in and kissed me so hard that it had Jay squirming in his chair again as he tried to break loose.

"Until we meet again," Ivan said, untying the last cord, then standing and walking off.

He had just reached the door when I reached over to untie Jay. "You need to calm down," I whispered, as I struggled with the rope.

"Calm down? That asshole kissed you right in front of me."

"Like you told me the other day, now's not the time." I finally got the rope around his arms untied and he jerked free, then darted toward the door.

"He's not going to just disrespect me like that!"

"Jay," I whispered, "where are you going? Do you want Max and his thugs to catch us?"

Jay stopped at the door as if common sense were prevailing.

I came up behind him. "You can't go after him. He's helping us, remember? They'll have us tied back up so fast, and who knows what else they'll do."

"Fine, whatever." Jay took his anger out on the concrete floor, stomping to the back of the room and the door Ivan had told us to exit out of. "Let's just go." He led the way out the door. Just like Ivan had said, there was a fire escape, which we took all the way down.

Jay took my hand and we ran for what seemed like ten minutes without seeing a soul. I just knew that at any moment Max or Will or someone was going to come up and drag us back into the SUV. Finally, we spotted a cab. After getting the driver to pull over, we jumped in, praying that we could make it to the seaplane and off this island without being spotted.

eighteen

J ay had paid cash for our seaplane tickets. This was
one of those times I was thankful for his pocketful of
cash he always carried. Luckily, the small airport
didn't seem up-to-date on security techniques and the
woman behind the counter didn't flinch when Jay said our
wallets and identification had been stolen. She just took our
money and passed the tickets. We'd boarded the seaplane
and made the twenty-minute flight back to Saint Thomas.
Just as Ivan instructed, we caught another cab to the airport
and prayed that we'd be able to get on a plane.

I spotted the Virgin baggage counter and nervously
walked over. "Excuse me, we're looking for Talib," I said, trying to appear casual.

The clerk pointed toward a three-hundred-pound man
who was dozing by the emergency exit in a wicker chair that
looked like it was about to collapse at any moment.

"Thank you." I motioned for Jay to follow me.

We tiptoed up on the man.

"Excuse me, Talib? I was told you could help us," Jay said, his voice low.

Talib barely looked up. "You got money?"

"All we have is about five hundred dollars," Jay replied. We'd actually gotten some cash from the ATM when we arrived at the airport, but we didn't know when or if police would cut off the credit and debit cards, so we'd discussed trying to hang on to some cash. Since I had stormed out of my hotel room with nothing but my room key, I had no access to cash.

"Come see me when you have money," Talib replied with a heavy accent.

"Look, we're good for it," Jay said. "But that's all we have on us. My wife doesn't have her purse and the ATM only lets us withdraw four hundred dollars a day."

Talib finally looked up, his eyes settling on Jay's Movado watch. "Four hundred, the watch"—he glanced at my hand—"and the ring."

"What? No way," Jay said, his hand instinctively covering my ring finger.

Talib shrugged. "Suit yourself." He leaned back and lowered his straw hat over his eyes.

"That's a fifteen-thousand-dollar ring," Jay protested.

"Like I said, suit yourself," Talib repeated.

I pulled the ring off my hand. "Here, take the ring. It's not like it means anything anyway," I said sharply.

"Shannon, what are you doing?" Jay pulled me toward him.

"Jay, we don't have room for negotiation." I motioned toward the flight billboard. "The flight to D.C. leaves in a few minutes and we need to be on it."

"No, we . . . we can go to the police," Jay said.

Talib let out a small chuckle from under his hat. "The people that you're running from, I'm sure they have the police in their pockets. You'll be here a very long time trying to work it all out."

Jay paused like he was trying to think of other options. "Okay, fine," he finally said, removing his watch. "But I'll be back for this ring."

"Why bother?" I muttered. After all we'd been through, a ring that obviously couldn't keep Jay true to his vows was the least of my concerns.

Jay handed Talib the money, the ring, and the watch, and Talib stood as if we weren't in a hurry and walked over to the Virgin ticket counter. He motioned to a girl pecking away at the computer. She walked over and he whispered something in her ear. She nodded, returned to her computer, and continued pecking. In a matter of minutes, she printed out two tickets and handed them to Talib.

"We don't have ID," I said when Talib returned and handed us the tickets, which said *Mr. and Mrs. Lawrence Cook.* I was relieved because I hadn't thought we'd be as lucky as we'd been in Saint Croix, especially since this airport was bigger.

"Just go to security, tell the guy there that Tiny said hi, then go get on the plane," Talib said.

I was skeptical, but we didn't have time to debate. Thankfully, the line for security moved quickly.

"Tiny said hi," Jay said, as he handed the TSA agent the tickets. The agent nodded, then ushered us through.

Ten minutes later, we were sitting in row 12 on board the plane.

"Are we gonna be okay?" I finally asked Jay, who looked just as nervous as I did.

"Yes," he said, squeezing my hand. He tried to sound confident, but an eerie feeling told me it would be a while before we were ever okay again.

nineteen

That had to have been the longest, scariest four hours of my life. I had ridden in fear, even as the plane sailed to thirty thousand feet. I knew that any minute it was going to turn around and land back in the Virgin Islands, and the police were going to drag me and Jay off it in handcuffs.

We'd been in the air for an hour before I was able to let go of even some of that fear and relax. Jay must've been worn out, just like me, because he didn't say much of anything for the entire plane ride. Either that or he was still thinking about Ivan.

I had never been so happy to see the D.C. skyline come into view. Both Jay and I had tensed up as we deplaned in Washington, fearful that the police would be waiting at the gate.

But no one had been waiting. Not at the gate, or when we walked out of the airport and to the valet to retrieve his vehicle.

Now we were in Jay's SUV, heading home. It wasn't until we pulled onto the freeway that I spoke.

"Do you think Ivan let us go on his own, or that they told him to let us go?" I asked, breaking the nervous tension that filled the SUV.

"Maybe being with you was just so good to him that he wanted to let you go so the two of you could meet up again." Jay didn't bother trying to hide his sarcasm.

I decided not to respond. I'd taken enough digs at him these last few days that I was going to allow him this one.

"Where are we going?" I said, when I noticed him pass the exit to our house. Or *my* house, since he hadn't been back there in more than five weeks.

Jay sat staring straight ahead, obviously still upset. He'd probably spent the whole plane ride thinking about me and Ivan. *Good*, I thought. Now he might understand what I felt.

Jay finally shook his head like he was trying to push away any thoughts of me and Ivan. "We're searching for answers, so we need to try to find this stupid jump drive they're talking about."

"And what are we going to do with it once we find it?"

"I don't know," Jay responded, exasperated. "But Ivan was right—unless we plan on staying on the run the rest of our lives, it's just a matter of time before those thugs from Saint Croix track us down. So we need to just find this drive, get these people off our backs, and hopefully clear our names since I'm sure they're going to try and pin Vonda's murder on us."

"And how are we going to do that?" This was never-ending.

"Shannon, it's like I said—I don't know. But I'm guessing we start at Vonda's house."

I cringed. "I'm sure you have a key so we don't have to break in or anything."

"Yes, I do have a key," he replied. "And it's a good thing or we'd be out of luck."

I let out a pained laugh. Was he purposely trying to hurt me? "But yet you want me to believe there was nothing to this relationship."

He kept his gaze straight ahead. "There really wasn't. Vonda insisted that I have the key, and taking it was easier than fighting her on it. I've never used it."

"Whatever, Jay," I said, folding my arms and turning to stare out the window. "Can we just go find this jump drive so we can get out of this mess, finalize our divorce, and get on with our lives?" I was exhausted, and fighting with Jay was the last thing I wanted to do right now.

Jay finally turned to look at me. And if I hadn't known any better, I would've thought I saw a flicker of regret. But Jay quickly turned his attention back to the road and we rode in silence until I found myself saying, "What happened? What made you stray?"

The tone of my voice must have gotten to him because he looked over at me, an apologetic expression on his face. He pulled off the freeway and into a parking lot. After cutting off the SUV's engine, he turned to face me. "Shannon, I'm sorry. I can't say that enough." He sighed. "If I'm being honest, I strayed because it got to the point that I hated where we were. I hated the constant fighting, the constant attitude. If I breathed too loud, you got mad. Any little thing I did aggravated you to no end, and there was just no joy left in our lives. I missed what we had. We used to laugh, enjoy life. When's the last time we had that? Then I felt like you had flipped the script and gotten mad at me because I didn't like your new rules."

"What do you mean by that?" I managed to ask, though his words pained me.

He let out another long sigh, like he had some stuff he'd been wanting to say but had been holding in.

"Shannon, we talked about our plans before we got married," he continued. "Not only that, we agreed on them. We said we weren't going to have kids. I had one kid out of wedlock—"

"But we're married, Jay," I interrupted.

"Please, let me finish," he huffed. I motioned for him to continue. "I hated Ericka for going behind my back and planning to get pregnant because she knew I was adamant about not wanting kids yet. So I missed out on the first three years of my daughter's life because I was being an asshole, harboring animosity, failing to realize Ericka hadn't gotten pregnant on her own. I was too busy being angry and trying to keep this singing career going to make time for my child, and when all was said and done, the career was over, and I wasn't even there when my child died."

In all our years of marriage, Jay had only talked twice about the child he'd lost, a little girl named Jamila who'd died in a car accident when she was seven. She'd been in a car with her nanny when they were hit by a drunk driver. The fact that neither Jay nor Ericka had been with their child when she died tore at his soul.

"I understand that," I said, my tone empathetic, "and I know it must've hurt you, but I don't see what that had to do with us."

He pounded the steering wheel. "Because you and I were both busy, wrapped up in our careers. I didn't want to bring another child into this world who might be neglected."

"So you don't think a child would've changed anything? That we wouldn't have made that child our priority?" I asked. Why had we never had this conversation before? Once I'd decided I wanted kids, I'd told him, he'd said no, and every conversation thereafter had been an argument.

"It wasn't a chance I was willing to take. I never wanted to go through the heartache of losing a child again." He exhaled slowly. "Besides, I was clear before we got married that I didn't want any more kids. And you agreed. You said you didn't want children. Then you just flipped the script. That . . . that's why I went and had the vasectomy."

"Without my knowledge."

"Just like you were going to stop taking your birth control pills without my knowledge." My eyes widened. How did he know that?

"I heard you on the phone with Nicole one day," he said, answering my silent question. "You thought I was gone. You told her you were going to sneak and stop taking them."

"But I didn't," I protested. "I was just venting!" I remembered that conversation because I'd really thought about it. I'd figured once Jay laid eyes on our precious child we'd be fine. But ultimately, I'd decided that was a level of deception I didn't want to go to.

Jay shrugged. "I didn't know that. All I knew was I didn't want to take that chance." He looked me in the eyes. "There would've been time, Shannon. You know all this notoriety and success is fleeting. We could've talked about it and taken some time, and maybe we could've come to some kind of agreement."

"We didn't have time to take," I said, a mist covering my eyes. Why had we both chosen deception as a way to deal with our issues? "Jay, you don't get it. My time is running out. I'm approaching forty."

"You're two years from forty," he replied. "And more and more women are having babies later in life. But the bottom line is you were okay with it before we got married. But it's like you just forgot about that. You changed your mind and decided you wanted a child and screw how I felt about it. You became consumed with it. So much so that it was all you talked about. And then when I didn't give you what you wanted, the part of you that's used to getting your way developed a permanent attitude. You know what it's like in this stressful field we're in. You think I like having to smile in these women's faces all day long?"

"Yeah, I do," I quipped.

"No, I don't," he said matter-of-factly. "It's a job. Remember, this has been my life since I was eighteen. And now that the book and show are doing so well, it's only getting worse with the women going overboard. I didn't want that. I wanted stability. I wanted peace. I wanted you. Those women throwing themselves at me back in the day, and even now, don't impress me. In fact, I'm tired of it. It's why I got married. I wanted to be a one-woman man."

"Humph," I said, rolling my eyes. "That's laughable."

He groaned. "See? That's exactly what I'm talking about." He turned to start the SUV. "Who wants to deal with this day in and day out? I don't even know why I bother trying to talk to you."

I reached out to touch his hand to keep him from turning the ignition. This was the first time we were having a heart-to-heart and I didn't want to mess it up with bitterness. "I'm sorry. You just have to understand, this whole thing hurts."

His chest rose, then fell as he released his grip on the key. "I do understand that and I am so, so sorry. But my point was I do what I have to do when it comes to the Lovejoy brand. We've built our success on this whole fixing-heartache-among-women act, and that's all it is—an act. At the end of the day, I just wanted to come home to relax and enjoy my wife. Instead, for the past year, I've come home to someone I love, but whom I no longer like."

That hurt, but I let him finish.

He continued. "I had to deal with my wife walking around with a chip on her shoulder, mad as hell, rationing sex because she decided to change the rules and I didn't want to play the game her way."

"So what? That gave you an excuse to go out and cheat?"

"No, it didn't," he replied. "I was wrong. I take responsibility for my actions. You didn't push me into the arms of another woman. That's a decision I made fully on my own. Would I have made that decision if you hadn't turned into this woman I couldn't stand?" He looked at me pointedly. "No. But that still doesn't make what I did right. I can apologize every single day to you. I know I was wrong. I should've just left before I got involved with Vonda."

I was quiet and pensive. "How did you meet her?"

"At Starbucks," he said. I could tell he didn't want to answer these questions, but I was glad he did. Finally. "We just started talking," Jay continued. "She said she used to be a fan."

"That's unlike you," I said. During his heyday, Jay had had a reputation for not crossing the line with groupies. Ericka, his daughter's mother, had been a groupie, and after she'd turned up pregnant, Jay had sworn that no one else would trap him like that again.

"I know." His voice was filled with regret. "I went against my better judgment, and I ended up with Psycho Sally."

"Did you invite her to the Virgin Islands?" Since Jay was opening up, maybe I could get some answers.

Jay shook his head. "No, Shannon. I swear, I would never do anything like that. She knew about the retreat just like everyone else did. I actually started pulling back from her long before you found out. The more I got to know her, the more unstable she seemed. She was obsessive and clingy. But every time I tried to walk away, she would go ballistic on me, and it just got to the point where it was just easier to pacify her, say what she wanted to hear, until I could figure out how to permanently get rid of her."

"Well, she's permanently gone now," I said, my mind returning to the fiasco we'd found ourselves in the middle of.

"Yeah, and I don't want to be blamed for that." Jay turned the SUV back on. "So let's go see what we can find out." He looked at me and, for the first time in a long time, smiled at me.

I returned his smile. "Thank you for your honesty. I'm glad we could talk."

I just wished we had done it a long time ago, I wanted to add. But I was at least grateful that I could get some closure.

twenty

fought back the bile rising in my throat. If I didn't get my emotions under control, I was going to throw up all over the floor. All the empathy I had been feeling toward my husband just thirty minutes earlier was out the window as we stood in the middle of Vonda's living room.

I glanced around the room once again. Never in a million years had I thought I'd be stepping into this . . . this shrine to Jay.

"I'm sorry," Jay said as he darted around the room, removing the pictures. Five-by-sevens, eight-by-tens, a poster from his first album. There had to be thirty pictures of Jay all over Vonda's home.

"Just how long were you seeing her again?" I asked as I slowly surveyed the room. I felt like my body was there, but my mind had been transported to another place, back to the place that fueled my anger and bitterness.

"I told you, it really wasn't that long. A couple of months."

He glanced around the room like he couldn't believe the sight himself. "I told you she was obsessive. I mean, half these pictures weren't here when I was seeing her, which means she added this stuff after I told her it was over."

This wasn't making sense. This chick had become obsessive, and Jay really wanted me to believe he was innocent in all this. "So you did nothing to encourage this?" I asked.

"Of course I did," he admitted. "I started it in the first place; then when I saw she was spazzing out on me, I tried to distance myself instead of just cutting her off. I told you I tried to take the easy way out."

"By avoiding the issue?" I knew that motif all too well. It was a quality about him that drove me crazy. It was part of why we hadn't discussed our own issues in detail.

"I . . . I'm sorry," Jay said as he scurried past me and turned more pictures facedown. But there was no way he could move fast enough to keep me from seeing the virtual shrine inside Vonda's apartment.

I followed Jay into the bedroom. It was obvious someone had beaten us here, as all of Vonda's drawers were hanging open and it looked like every crevice had been inspected. But despite all the mess, all I could focus on were the pictures— pictures that were everywhere. Of Jay by himself. Of Jay and Vonda at the park, eating ice cream, attending some type of function, selfies that she had blown up and had printed.

I picked up a photo of Vonda holding Jay's three-year-old niece, Meghan.

A lump formed in my throat. "Y-you took her around

Meghan?" was all I could say. Meghan was my heart and joy. She filled the void of the child Jay and I had yet to conceive. And he'd had the audacity to bring another woman around her?

"It's not what it seems," Jay mumbled.

How in the hell could he even fix his lips to say that?

"Really, Jay? That's your response?"

"Shannon . . . seriously, Vonda followed me one weekend when I took Meghan to the park. She just showed up."

"Who is this man?" I said, holding up a picture of Jay and thrusting it in his face. "Because the Jay that I knew," I continued, fighting back tears, "he could be a little arrogant, and even a little chauvinistic from time to time, but I would've never believed he was capable of this."

Jay was usually confident, but at this moment, he simply looked defeated. "It really wasn't—"

"Did you love her?"

"Shannon, let's not do this," he pleaded.

"Did you love her?" I screamed.

He released an exasperated sigh. "No, I didn't. I swear to God."

"So you ruined our life over some chick you don't even love?"

Jay didn't even bother trying to respond.

"Did you ever tell her you loved her?"

"No," he said, running his hands over his head. "But she told me."

"And what did you say?"

"Nothing. That's part of the problem, I never said anything." He stepped to me and tried to take my hands. "But, baby, we've got to stay focused. We've got to find out what it is these people are talking about. Vonda is gone, and unless we figure all of this out, we can find ourselves paying the price for that."

"Right, and I'm caught up in the middle of all this drama because of you." I snatched my hands away and hit his chest. And before I knew it, I couldn't stop. I pummeled his chest with a flurry of fists. "Why did you do this to me? To us?" I cried.

"I'm sorry, I'm sorry," he repeated, as he pulled me toward him.

"You sure are," I cried. "How could you do this to me?"

I sobbed as he held me tightly, rocking back and forth, caressing my hair and mumbling "I'm sorry" over and over.

We stayed that way for what felt like ten minutes, me crying and Jay trying to console me. I hadn't really meant to get so emotional, but the weight of everything we'd been through—of all that I was seeing now—had simply taken its toll.

We were interrupted by the sound of the ringing telephone. Both of us stared at the home phone until it stopped ringing and Vonda's answering machine popped on. I hadn't even known people still used answering machines.

Vonda's greeting played; then a voice said, "Hey, it's Keri. Where are you? I am so worried about you. I don't have a good vibe about this, and maybe this whole plan needs to be dropped. These are some dangerous people. Give me a call. I'm going nuts over here. I need to hear from you."

Jay jumped to pick up the phone. "Keri?" It was too late. She had already hung up.

"Who is Keri?" I said, as Jay hung the phone back up.

"That's Vonda's best friend. I just thought maybe she could give us some insight into what's going on."

Jay picked up the handset again and pressed a button.

"What are you doing?" I asked.

"I'm calling her back."

"Put me on speakerphone," I demanded.

Jay did as I asked. Keri answered on the first ring. "Oh my God, Vonda, where have you been?"

"It's not Vonda."

Silence filled the phone.

"Keri, it's Jay."

"I know who it is. What are you doing calling me from Vonda's phone? Where is she?"

Jay paused. "Look, Keri, I need to know what's going on. What kind of dangerous game do you think Vonda was caught up in?"

"Why are you in her apartment? Where is Vonda?" Keri's voice was filled with panic.

"Keri, what are you talking about? What plan?"

She hesitated, then her tone turned flippant. "I don't know what you're talking about."

"Keri, you said these people are dangerous. What people? What was Vonda into?"

Keri paused, then rushed her words out. "Do you know where she is? She needs to get out of town. They came up to my job looking for her, and my neighbor said she'd seen two men in my apartment."

"Well, someone has definitely been here too," Jay said.

"See, I told Vonda she was playing with fire. You've got to convince her to get out of town. Where is she?"

Jay was quiet as he exchanged glances with me. Finally, he said, "Keri, Vonda is dead. She was murdered in the Virgin Islands."

Keri gasped. "Noooo!" she cried. "No, no, no," she kept repeating.

"Keri, I need you to calm down." Sobs continued to fill the phone.

"Where are you?" Jay asked.

The phone went dead.

I was just about to ask whether he should've revealed so much to this Keri woman when someone banged on the front door of the apartment.

"Vonda, is that you?" a voice called out from the other side. "It's Mrs. Murphy. Open the door, I need to talk to you. There've been some funny people creeping around here and I don't like that. I told you I don't condone all this foolishness up in my place." She pounded on the door again. "Plus, you owe me this month's rent. I'm tired of you being late, then trying to avoid me. I'm gonna use my key," she threatened.

Jay and I froze, unsure of what to do. "Come on," he said, pulling me toward the window. He jimmied the window open and both of us climbed through it and outside onto a patio area. We'd just pulled the window closed when the front door flew open. An elderly woman with graying hair and a pink-and-purple housecoat stuck her head in the door. I didn't see much after that because Jay and I hightailed it back to the SUV.

"We'll just have to try again later," Jay said, once we were safely sitting back in his vehicle.

My heart was racing like I'd run a 10K. "We're not trying anything," I snapped, shaking my head in exasperation. "We're going to the police."

"We're wanted for murder." He turned to face me. "Are you willing to have our name dragged through the mud while we try to prove we didn't kill someone?"

I rubbed my temple, wishing we could go back to when the highlight of our day was laughing about callers and their problems.

"We don't know if police are even looking for us," I said.

"We don't know that they're not," Jay replied. "And if they're not, it's just a matter of time."

I leaned back in the seat and folded my arms. I couldn't believe this.

"It's bad enough I have to think about what you did, now I have to figure out how to dodge the police too?" My voice cracked at the same time a pounding filled my head.

He sighed. "Shannon, we're going to work all of this out."

"Just take me home, Jay."

"We can't go home," he said solemnly.

That revelation was like a sledgehammer removing the wall holding up the dam. I buried my face in my hands and sobbed as I wondered how in the world my life had spiraled into this madness.

twenty-one

"So where are we heading?" I asked after I pulled myself together. We'd been driving for ten minutes and I had no idea where Jay was going. I knew one thing: I was ready to go home, get out of these clothes, bathe, get in my bed, and sleep until all this madness was solved.

"We're going to see Vonda's friend and try to get to the bottom of what's going on." Jay kept his eyes focused on the road as he pulled onto the freeway. I didn't say anything else because all I could think was that Jay knew the way to Keri's place, which meant he'd been there before. It hurt that Jay had not only cheated on me but was apparently chummy with his mistress's friends. He wanted me to believe the relationship had been meaningless, but he had integrated himself into Vonda's life.

I debated saying something but decided against it. I didn't want to know any more about this relationship. I just wanted to get out of this trouble, then get as far away from Jay as I possibly could.

When we arrived at a large apartment building, Jay swung his SUV into a private parking space and got out.

"Are you coming?" he leaned in and asked when I didn't move. "Or do you just want to continue this silent treatment and let me handle this myself?"

I released an exasperated breath as I followed him out of the vehicle and up the stairs to a second-floor apartment. Jay put a finger over the peephole, then knocked.

"Who is it?" a voice called out.

Jay lowered his voice. "It's Charlie, from downstairs."

I folded my arms and glared. *He knew neighbors too?*

Keri opened the front door, then quickly tried to shut it when she realized it wasn't Charlie.

"Go away!" she cried.

Jay put his foot in the door to stop her from closing it all the way. "I need to talk to you," he said.

Keri pushed on the door, trying desperately to close it, but Jay's Timberland boots made it virtually impossible.

"I did my research," Keri said through the crack in the door. "Police think you're the one who killed Vonda. It's in the Virgin Islands paper."

So the police were looking for us.

"Keri, you know better than that!" Jay declared.

"I don't know anything!" She kicked at his foot as she struggled to close the door.

I don't know what came over me, but I kicked the door with all my might and sent Keri tumbling back.

I bogarted my way inside. "Look, we don't have time for

these games!" I jabbed my finger in the face of the petite woman with flyaway hair.

"Who the hell are you?" Keri asked, backing up against the wall as her eyes darted around like she was looking for something to use as a weapon.

"I'm the pissed-off wife." I stepped close to Keri's face as Jay followed me in and closed the door. "Your bimbo friend and my no-good husband have gotten me caught up in all this drama and I need to get to the bottom of it. Now, if you know something, we need to know it."

"Look, lady, I don't have anything to do with this," Keri said, her voice trembling. The bravado she'd displayed previously was gone.

"But you do," I said, stepping even closer to show the woman I meant business. I wasn't a fighter, but with all the rage built up inside me right about then, I probably could have knocked out Mike Tyson. "And I want to know what the hell is going on."

Jay stepped in front of me, almost as if he knew I was a ticking time bomb about to explode.

"Keri, I'm sorry, but I hope you can understand, my wife is pretty worked up. Someone is trying to frame us for Vonda's murder and we didn't do it. You know we didn't do it."

"I don't know nothing," she said, her eyes darting back and forth between the two of us.

"Keri, please, just help us try to figure out what's going on. Some very bad guys tried to kidnap us. We managed to get away, but I doubt they'll just go away. If the police do pick us up, that means the real killers are still out there."

"And they may try to tie up all the loose ends, including friends that they think may know something," I added.

Keri wrung her hands nervously, then let out a deep sigh as a lone tear trickled down her cheek.

"I told Vonda these people were dangerous," she said softly, more to herself than to us. "She wouldn't listen."

"Who are 'these people'?" Jay asked.

"I don't want to get involved in this." She looked terrified.

"You already are involved," Jay said. His voice was calm, like he was really trying to get through to her. "Just tell us what you know; then we'll leave."

Keri wiped her face and took a deep breath before continuing. "I don't know if they killed her or not, but I do know she was playing a very dangerous game."

"With whom? Who is 'they'?" I demanded.

Jay shot me a *Let me talk* look. I retreated, but didn't bother to hide my scowl. We didn't have time to be babying this woman.

The woman cut her eyes at me but continued talking to Jay. "You ever heard of Bradley Bell?"

Jay paused like he was searching his memory. "The senator?" he finally said.

"Yeah, that one." It was obvious she held monumental disdain for Senator Bell.

"What about him?"

"Was Vonda sleeping with him too?" I asked.

Keri smirked at Jay like she didn't mind delivering that piece of news.

"What do you think?" she said.

Jay looked shocked, and I didn't miss his expression. I actually took small comfort in the surprise on his face. All this crap Vonda had been spewing—now Jay knew his wasn't the only ego she'd been feeding.

Jay shook off his surprise. "Why would Bradley want Vonda dead, though?"

"Look, I've already said too much." Keri headed toward the door and held it open. "You have to go."

Keri's phone, which sat on the mantel next to me, rang. I glanced down and saw *Westhaven Nursing Home* on the caller ID. Keri muttered a curse word as she darted over and grabbed the phone.

"Hello," she said, turning her back to us. "Is my grandmother okay . . . ?" She stepped off to the side and lowered her voice, and I did a mental scan of her living room. Unlike at Vonda's, the pictures in Keri's place were scarce, with the exception of a photo of Keri standing over the bed of an older woman, holding a birthday cake. There was a stack of mail on the table and I eased over to steal a glance. I had no idea what I was looking for, but I wanted to see if I could find out any information about Vonda.

There were a lot of overdue bills and a notice from Westhaven Nursing Home. I strained to get a glimpse but only saw the first line—*We're writing in regard to your grandmother, Eloise Walker*—before Keri stomped over and snatched the papers up.

"Let me call you back," she said into the phone. "What are you doing?" she shouted at me.

"Nothing, I . . . umm, I was just . . ."

"You were just digging where you don't have any business." She pointed toward the door. "I'm going to ask you again: please leave before I call the police."

Jay gently grabbed Keri's arm. "Keri, please. What does Bradley Bell have to do with this?"

She hesitated, shot daggers my way, then said, "Vonda discovered some information that Bradley didn't want getting out."

"What was this information?" Jay asked.

"I don't know. She wouldn't tell me. But I know that in the last few days it had her spooked. I suggested she leave town for a little bit, and she said she had the perfect place to go."

"Yeah, she came to the Virgin Islands, following her lover," I interjected.

Jay sucked his bottom lip but kept his attention focused on Keri. "So you have no idea what she had on him?"

She shifted her eyes downward.

"Keri, I need to know," he pleaded, grabbing her tighter.

"Fine!" She snatched her arm out of his grip. "Just wait a minute." She retreated to her bedroom.

We stood in the living room, a cloak of silence blanketing us.

Finally, I spoke. "As soon as this is over and we get our lives back, I want you to sign the divorce papers."

"Don't act like you've been Dolly Do-Right," Jay snapped. "Don't forget, you have a skeleton of your own."

"Well, we're not accused of murdering *my* lover."

He flinched at the reference to Ivan.

"Yeah, it hurts, doesn't it?" I continued. "The idea of me being intimate with someone else tears at your insides, huh? Try the idea of someone else being obsessively *in love* with me. How would that make you feel? And then she's sleeping with Bradley Bell and God only knows who else. My God. I need to be tested for HIV," I said. That thought made me ill, and I shook it off so I could focus for now. "What's taking her so long?"

Before Jay could answer, Keri walked back into the room. "I don't know what's in here," she said, handing Jay a manila envelope. "I didn't want to know. All I know is Vonda said if anything ever happens to her, to open this."

"Why didn't you open it?" he asked, taking the envelope.

"Number one, I didn't know anything had happened to her until you just told me, and number two, whatever is in there probably got Vonda killed and I don't want to know." She looked at the envelope like it carried some sort of plague.

"Fine," Jay said, flipping the envelope over to open it.

Keri stopped him. "Unh-unh. Take it and get out of my place. I still don't want to know. Just take it and go."

"Okay." Jay headed toward the door. I was close behind him. We stepped outside and he turned around. "Thank you, Keri. I promise we're going to find out who did this."

Keri slammed the door without responding.

twenty-two

Jay and I barely made it into the SUV before he was ripping the envelope open. He started silently reading the letter. I pushed his shoulder.

"Read it out loud!" I demanded.

"Oh, I wasn't thinking," Jay said. "It says, 'Keri, I hope you never have a reason to open this. But if you're reading this, that's not a good sign. Don't let them get away with this. The stuff they want is—'" He abruptly stopped reading.

"The stuff they want is what?" I asked.

He swallowed, then continued reading. "The stuff they want is with Jay. Make sure he takes it to the cops. Love you, Vonda."

"What stuff do you have?" I eyed him suspiciously. "I thought you didn't know what was going on."

"I don't," he protested. His brow furrowed in confusion. "I have no idea what Vonda is talking about."

"Well, let's go back and talk to Keri."

"No way she opens the door again." Jay shook his head and pulled out his work cell phone from the glove compartment. He turned it on and punched in a number, and I couldn't help but note that he had it memorized.

"I remembered the number from Vonda's phone," he said, as if he were reading my mind.

I just stared at him. At this point, I couldn't distinguish lies from truth.

"Keri, wait, don't hang up. . . . I know, I won't bother you anymore but I have to ask: this note from Vonda says I have the stuff they want. What is Vonda talking about? . . . Uh-huh . . . Please, I'm not trying to cause problems. Just tell me." He paused for a few seconds, then said, "But I don't . . ." He moved the phone away from his ear and faced me. "She hung up."

"What did she say?"

He sighed in frustration. "She claims she doesn't know. The only thing she would say was that Vonda alluded to sending something important to me. She thinks that might be it."

"Sent *what* to you?"

"I. Don't. Know. Vonda has never sent me anything." He hesitated like he was deep in thought. "Wait a minute . . ." He tossed the phone on the console and started the SUV. "I think I may have an idea what she's talking about."

Jay pulled the SUV out into traffic. I pummeled him with questions, but he would only respond with "Just give me a minute, I'm trying to think."

I leaned back in the seat and crossed my arms. This whole

James Bond caper was getting on my nerves. I just wanted to go back to my normal life. "At least tell me where we're going," I finally said.

"To the radio station."

"For what?"

"Just bear with me."

"So we're just going on a wild-goose chase based off something Keri said? She's shifty. There's something about her that I don't trust."

"Right now, Shannon, Keri is our only lead, so let's just see what we can find out."

I wanted to scream, but I remained quiet as I settled back in the seat. Fifteen minutes later, we were pulling into the radio station.

"We're gonna have to move quick. I doubt the police here are vigilantly looking for us yet, but we can't take any chances."

Jay used his card key to go in the back entrance of the station. I was grateful that the only person who saw us was Ed, the old, useless security guard.

We quietly made our way up the stairwell to the third floor, where the offices were located.

"Can you tell me what you're looking for?" I asked, once we were in Jay's office.

Jay pulled a box out from under his desk. He dug through some tapes and magazines. "This," he said, holding up a teddy bear. "Vonda sent me this crazy-looking Build-A-Bear teddy. I thought it was strange, but I didn't pay it any attention and just tossed it in a box." He flipped the bear over and dug inside.

I was just about to ask him what lie he would have told me if I'd seen the bear, but the intense expression on his face stopped me.

"Bingo," Jay said, holding up a small flash drive. "Obviously, whatever Vonda was holding over the senator is on this," he said, turning his computer on.

We stood anxiously as we waited for the computer to power up. Jay popped the drive in, and within seconds, several Microsoft Excel documents filled the screen.

"What's all that?" I asked, leaning in next to him. Even after two days on the run and the nightmare we'd been through, my husband still smelled good.

"I have no idea," Jay replied, scrolling down the page.

I shook away my thoughts. Why the hell was I thinking about his smell?

"'Land-Acquisition Plan,'" Jay said, reading the title. "It just looks like some real estate stuff. I can't make sense of any of this. It's just a bunch of numbers. . . . Wait a minute, what is this?" he said, zooming in on the page.

"This is highlighted. 'Payment to Richard Holmes and Lance DeMontrond for N.O. levee plan,'" I read. "Two hundred fifty thousand dollars. Wow."

"I assume N.O. is New Orleans, the senator's home district, but who are Richard Holmes and Lance DeMontrond?" Jay said.

"I don't know, but we need to find out," I said, sliding into the seat at his assistant's desk. I logged onto the assistant's computer. "I'll look up Lance and Richard and you keep looking through that and see what you can find."

All it took was a quick Google search and I was led to the official City of New Orleans web page. I scrolled through the departments. "Okay, got it. Lance is the city inspector and Richard is with the U.S. Army Corps of Engineers." I leaned back in the seat. "Why would the senator be paying them?"

Jay continued studying his screen. "Maybe because of this," he finally said, his eyes wide at his discovery.

I stood and walked around to Jay's side of the desk. On the computer screen was an artist's rendition of a massive casino complex.

"So what? It's another casino. Doesn't New Orleans already have one?" I said.

He scrolled down the page. "Yeah, but look at where they're trying to build this one," Jay said, a look of disbelief on his face.

"Where? I can't tell anything from this map," I said, leaning in closer to survey the screen.

"You know my buddy Jerome is from New Orleans, so I'm kind of familiar with the city, and this," Jay said, pointing to the middle of the casino drawing, "is smack-dab in the middle of the Ninth Ward."

"How are they going to build a casino in the middle of a neighborhood?" I asked.

Jay leaned back, confused. "I have no idea."

"Hey," I said, an idea hitting me. "Nicole won an Edward R. Murrow Award for a segment she produced on Hurricane Katrina and New Orleans when she was working for the *Washington Post*. So she did a lot of research." I picked up the phone and started dialing. "Maybe she can give us an idea as to what this all means. I just hope she answers."

Nicole picked up the phone on the second ring. "Hey, Nicole. It's me."

"Oh my God, Shannon!" she exclaimed. "Where are you?"

"We're safe. We're back in the States."

"What the hell is going on? You just up and left all your stuff here and disappeared in the middle of the conference." She was talking a mile a minute. "At first, I thought you made your flight, but the driver said you never showed. I thought something had happened to you guys until I found out the police are looking for you because they think you had something to do with Vonda's murder. Please tell me you didn't have anything to do with Vonda's murder."

"Come on, Nicole. You know better than that," I said.

"Shannon, what is going on? I talked with Emerson. He said you guys were on the news in D.C. tonight. Police there say you're wanted for murder."

"Calm down," I said, trying to take my own advice. Which was hard, since I felt nauseated in the pit of my stomach. We had made the local news. This nightmare, which it felt like we'd been living for days, instead of twenty-four hours, was about to get worse. "It's a very long story," I continued. "But you know we didn't kill anyone."

"I know that, and that's what I told the cops. But the fact that you and Jay are missing doesn't look good. And I'm not even going to tell you how furious the Family First Foundation is. Quincy is losing his mind."

I couldn't deal with the Family First Foundation or Quincy right now. "Nicole, I need you to just trust us on this. Jay and I were kidnapped at gunpoint."

"Kidnapped?" she exclaimed, then paused. "So that's the story we're rolling with?" she said.

"Nicole, I'm dead serious," I said. "We managed to get away and get off the island before these dudes killed us. We've gotten caught up in the middle of some major drama." Even as I was relaying the story, it sounded ludicrous. Unless we got to the bottom of this, no one would ever believe us.

"What kind of drama?" Nicole asked, panic clearly setting in.

"I don't have time to go into details," I said. "I just need to ask you some questions about New Orleans."

"New Orleans?" Nicole said, like she'd heard me wrong. "Are you serious? You're a wanted fugitive and you want to ask me questions about New Orleans?"

I finally got Nicole quiet long enough to fill her in on everything we'd found on the jump drive.

"So what do you think it means?" I asked when I was done. I looked over at Jay. He looked like he was dying to know what Nicole was saying.

"Hold on, Nicole, I'm putting you on speaker." I pushed the button for speaker and Nicole continued talking.

"I don't know what the hell is going on, but from what you've told me about this spreadsheet, this could be major," she said. "The Army Corps of Engineers has rebuilt the one hundred sixty-nine miles of levees, floodwalls, and gates that were damaged by hurricanes Katrina and Rita. Those areas were repaired to pre-Katrina design specs, some of them even stronger."

"But why would anyone need to be paid off for that? That's what everyone wants," Jay said.

"Shannon said there was a circle drawn around a portion of the drawing that said New Orleans East," Nicole said.

"Yeah," Jay replied. "It's actually an area five miles square."

"New Orleans East is in the Ninth Ward."

"Yeah, we know that. But what we don't understand," I said, "is what this all means."

Nicole sounded like she was getting excited. As a producer, she usually did when she was on the cusp of a big story. "Think about it. You said they're trying to build a casino. Real estate in New Orleans is through the roof. If you wanted to build a casino, or anything else, it could cost you millions." She paused. "Unless you can find some property that is valued at little or nothing."

Both Jay and I leaned back as the realization of what Nicole was saying set in.

"And one more disaster even close to Hurricane Katrina, and the Ninth Ward wouldn't recover?" Jay finally asked.

"Right," Nicole replied. "And if Mother Nature won't send another Katrina, you create one by building substandard levees and waiting on the first heavy rainstorm. The levees will break and you'll have catastrophic flooding. Again. Property values would plummet and the government would basically give the land away."

Jay shook his head in disbelief. "And guess who would swoop right in and buy up all the property?"

"Who?" Nicole asked.

Jay and I exchanged glances. I had conveniently left out

the senator's name, telling Nicole only that all of this was related to clearing our names. It was obvious Senator Bell was dangerous, and we didn't want to get Nicole any more involved than she already was. "We'll tell you all about it later."

"Shannon, what in the world is going on? Why are you guys playing investigative reporters when you're wanted for murder?" Nicole asked.

"Nicole, trust me, it'll all make sense soon. But right now, the less you know, the better."

"Shannon . . ."

"I'll get back in touch with you soon, okay?"

Nicole sighed. "Be careful. And let me know if there's anything I can do. Both Quincy and I will be back in D.C. tomorrow. We got your stuff packed up, and it's being shipped home too. We're trying to avoid the media vultures but they are everywhere, so you might want to stay offline."

"Thanks so much, Nic. And don't worry, we'll be safe. I don't have my phone, but we have Jay's work phone and we'll call you as soon as we can." I hung up and turned to Jay. "Okay, this is major. No wonder Vonda was blackmailing the senator. There's no way he'd want something like this to get out."

Jay nodded. "Yeah, it's reason enough for him to kill to keep it from coming out."

"Well, now that we know what this is all about, the question is, what do we do with this information?"

twenty-three

How in the world had I been thrust into the middle of a Lifetime espionage movie?

"Now what do we do?" I asked my husband. We were sitting in IHOP, supposedly to eat and discuss our next move. But neither of us had touched our pancakes. I was shocked that we hadn't crashed from exhaustion but the adrenaline from trying to stay alive must've been fueling us.

"Now we go see Bradley," Jay said bluntly.

I leaned into the table and lowered my voice. "Oh, yeah, right. We're just going to waltz up into his congressional office and tell him all the dirt we have on him." I threw up my hands. "Hello, do you hear yourself? First of all, we're not going to even make it past the lobby area. Secondly, like he's just going to admit to something this huge."

Jay held up the jump drive. "We have the evidence."

I shook my head. No way would this be that easy. Obviously, my husband never watched Lifetime. "Why don't we just take that to the cops?" I asked.

"Okay, we do that and we're able to prove that the senator is into some shady, Watergate-type stuff. But there's nothing to tie him to Vonda's death, and that's what we need to be concerned with. If what's on here is true, Bradley Bell will make sure he discredits us and that we go down for Vonda's murder. And there's no telling who a man that powerful has in his pocket. No, our best bet is to just give him the drive, let him know we don't want to be involved, and get him to clear our names."

"It's just that simple, huh?"

Jay exhaled his frustration. "I don't know if it'll work or not, but right now, it's all we got."

"How do we even know he's tied to those thugs in the Virgin Islands?" I asked. "I mean, are we really to believe Vonda had seduced the senator to the point that he'd share his illegal activities with her?"

"Vonda was crafty. I doubt he shared anything. She might have stumbled on it."

I shook my head, unconvinced.

"Nothing else makes sense," Jay said. "After what we saw on this drive, the senator is the only one behind this."

I knew the senator was the only one with the money and power to chase Vonda all over the place.

"So we just need to get in touch with the senator and play let's-make-a-deal, and when he clears our names, we give him the jump drive," Jay continued.

"I don't like this. We're just supposed to let the man create another natural disaster so he can build a freakin' casino?
Do we want that on our consciences?" I asked. "Remember
how many people died in Hurricane Katrina? Could you live
with that happening again and knowing we could've done
something?"

Jay slammed his hand on the table. "I just want to live our
lives, Shannon." He lowered his voice when the waitress
looked our way. "We turn this info over to the police and we'll
never see it again, and lose all hope of clearing our names."

My resolve weakened. I knew Jay was right. "So the question remains, how are we going to get in to see the senator?"

Jay paused like he was thinking. "Quincy will help get us
in," he finally said. "We need to call him."

Before I could reply, Jay quickly leaned in and kissed me
across the table.

"What the hell are you doing?" I asked, trying to pull away.

"Shhh," he said, motioning toward the door with his eyes.
I turned around and glanced at the two police officers who
had just walked in. I quickly turned back around. Nicole had
said the cops in D.C. were looking for us as well. We couldn't
take a chance on getting spotted.

"Let's just ease out as soon as they take their seats," Jay
whispered.

I had never felt so nervous. What if we were caught? The
very real possibility that I could go to jail for a crime I hadn't
committed filled my head. And even if we were eventually
exonerated, I'd have to go through a living nightmare first.

Luckily, one officer went to the bathroom in the rear of the restaurant and the other slid into a booth with his back to us. Jay stood, threw some money on the table, then grabbed my hand and led me out.

We didn't say anything until we were several blocks away, parked in the lot at a Target store.

"I can't take this, Jay," I finally mumbled.

"That's why we've got to handle this," he said as he pulled out his phone. He punched in a number, then put the phone on speaker. "I'm calling Quincy."

The phone rang twice, then Quincy's voice filled the SUV.

"Jay, man," he said, his voice filled with relief. "Where are you guys? I've been worried sick. What the hell is going on? Why haven't you been answering your phone? You just disappeared from Saint Thomas and the next thing I know, you're wanted for murder. What happened?"

"We're fine, Quincy. Shannon is here with me. I have you on speakerphone."

"The police in the Virgin Islands and D.C. are about to issue a warrant for your arrest. So can you tell me what in the world is going on?"

"Man, you know I didn't kill anybody," Jay said, repeating what had become our tagline. "Vonda was caught up in some real crooked stuff, and now I'm right in the middle of it."

"What kind of crooked stuff? And why didn't you bring this to me and we could just take this to the cops?"

"You said it yourself—I'm wanted for murder. I'm sure my fingerprints are in her room. And the people I think are responsible don't play around. If they want me to go down for murder, I go down for murder. Thanks, but no thanks."

Quincy was silent as Jay's words registered in his head. "What people, Jay? Tell me what in the world is going on."

Jay paused. "I can't say just yet."

Quincy exhaled an exasperated sigh. "So what, do you plan to stay on the run?"

"No, we're going to find the real killers," Jay replied.

"Okay, Perry Mason. You're no private eye, so don't go trying to dig for answers. Let the police do their job."

I could picture Quincy, his brow furrowed, his mind racing as he tried to figure out how he could fix this.

"Quincy, you remember when Joe got arrested for assaulting that woman in his building?" Jay said, referring to their old high school buddy.

"Yeah, what does that have to do with anything? He was exonerated."

"Yeah, but after spending six months in jail. I'm not trying to go out like that." Jay blew a frustrated breath. "You know what, just save it. My time is limited. I just need to know what you know about Bradley Bell."

"Who?"

"Bradley Bell, the senator from Louisiana."

"What does he have to do with anything?" Quincy asked.

I was tired of playing twenty questions, so I spoke up. "Do you know how to get in touch with him?"

"Why would I know that?"

"You're a high-profile attorney. You ought to know someone who knows him. What the hell are we paying you all this money for if you can't help us," I snapped.

"Look," Jay said, placing a hand on my arm in an effort to calm me, "Shannon didn't mean to get smart with you, but as you can imagine, we're freaking out over here. We're exhausted and running on pure adrenaline."

Quincy hesitated. "I understand, but I just don't . . . Wait, there's this one guy I went to law school with. He used to work in Senator Bell's office. I could see if he's still there."

"I need you to get in touch with him and set up a meeting ASAP."

I could hear his doubt as he said, "Bradley Bell is a well-known politician and the word is that he's going to be on the next presidential ticket. So the last thing he wants to be doing is having clandestine meetings with a wanted fugitive."

"Oh, I assure you, he'll want to meet with us," Jay said.

Silence, then, "Okay, Jay, you need to tell me what's going on."

"Just tell the senator that Vonda Howard passed his information on to me."

"Vonda, the dead woman? What does she have to do with anything?" Quincy asked. "What information did she have? Is that why she's dead?"

"Again, I'll explain everything later. For now, just do this for me. I'll call you back first thing in the morning."

"But, Jay—"

"No buts, Quincy. Just work this out for me."

Quincy let out a heavy sigh. "Okay, man, but I hope you know what you're doing."

"I don't have much choice. We'll be in touch." Jay pressed the end button to disconnect the call.

"So now what?" I asked.

"Now we wait," Jay replied, as he leaned back his seat to get comfortable.

twenty-four

had only been half-kidding when I said it felt like I was in a movie, but that's exactly where I was, only these weren't fictitious characters, and if they didn't figure out something, there definitely wouldn't be any happily-ever-after ending.

"What are you doing?" Jay asked as I dug in my bag for the cell phone I'd grabbed from the radio station. I downloaded my contacts and info from the cloud and saw tons of messages.

"I tell you what I'm *not* about to do. I'm not about to sit in the Target parking lot for God knows how long. We can't go home, because the police may be there, and if the police aren't there, some thugs may be there, and I just want to lie down," I huffed. "I'm calling Nicole. She has a condo downtown that I think is empty. Maybe we can go there until we figure all of this out." I was thankful Jay didn't protest as I punched in Nicole's number.

"Hey, Nicole."

"Hey, Shannon, are you guys okay? I've been going crazy since I talked to you. You guys really sound like you're in some kind of danger."

"We are," I confessed. "But we'll be okay."

"What's going on, Shannon? I need you to tell me everything. They're talking about murder, warrants. All the media is covering it. It's gone national. They said either you or Jay killed that woman Vonda."

I fell back against the headrest. "You know that as much as I would've loved to have strangled her until she begged for mercy, I didn't touch her." I looked over at Jay, who sat staring as if he was unsure whether he should comfort me. "And Jay may be a low-down, filthy, dirty dog, but he's not a killer."

He seemed relieved to hear those words coming from my mouth.

"So what's going on?" Nicole asked.

"Somebody killed her, all right, and they're trying to pin it on us. So we're trying to find out who."

"What do you mean find out who? You need to be letting the police do that."

"Nicole, we can't do that, especially now that we've run. We look guilty. We believe the person responsible is a powerful man. He'd make sure we rotted in jail."

Nicole gasped. "Person responsible? Who are you talking about? Is this all connected to the New Orleans stuff?"

I was just about to reply when the look in Jay's eyes stopped me. He shook his head, a warning that I was saying too much. "Hopefully, I'll be able to tell you all about it later. I don't want to get you involved any more than you already are. We just wanted to see if we can stay at your downtown condo."

"Dang, I rented it out last week, someone is in there."

"Aww, man, we're exhausted, but we can't go home."

"Yeah, I know. There were all kinds of newspeople at the station today. They're all over the place. I'm sure they're camped out at your place too."

"What are we gonna do?" My voice was panicked yet weary.

"Look, calm down. You can stay at my brother's apartment in Richmond. He's a college student, so it won't be much, but he's out of town. He has a spare key on the back porch."

"Oh, thank goodness, it's just for a day or two. Hopefully, we can get to the bottom of this and clear our names."

Nicole gave me directions and some more pertinent information. "Girl, you call me if you need anything."

"Thank you, Nicole. I love you."

"I love you too."

I hung up the phone and the river of tears was released. No longer hesitating, Jay took me into his arms and held me while I cried. After a few minutes, I began trying to pull myself together. This was getting ridiculous. I'd cried more in the past few days than I had in the past twenty years.

"I'm okay," I said, wiping my eyes. "I just want to go. Nicole said we can go to her brother Robert's place."

I put the address into the navigation system and we hit

the freeway. I was surprised that I actually fell asleep on the ride there. But the past few days had obviously taken their toll and I was utterly exhausted.

I woke to Jay gently shaking my leg. "Come on, babe. We're here."

I stretched, glanced around to make sure no one was nearby, and then stepped out of the vehicle.

I unlocked the door to the apartment and we made our way inside and got situated. Robert had an old beat-up chocolate sofa, but I plopped down on it and it felt like I was relaxing on a luxurious mattress.

"You hungry?" Jay asked, heading toward the kitchen.

"I am absolutely starving," I replied, suddenly wishing that I had devoured those pancakes.

I closed my eyes and inhaled deeply. The smell of gym socks didn't even bother me. I was just grateful for a place to lay my head.

"You can tell we're dealing with a college kid," Jay called out from the kitchen. I pulled myself up off the sofa and made my way to the kitchen.

"Why do you say that?" I leaned against the doorway.

"Let's see, we got Lunchables, beer, old pizza, or this unidentifiable object." He held up a clear plastic container with some type of yellowish pasta.

"Yeah, um, I'm gonna pass," I said.

Jay put the stuff back in the refrigerator, then walked over and opened the cabinet. "There's some chicken noodle soup here. You want that?"

I was just about to say no when my stomach answered for me.

"I guess that's a yes," Jay said.

I nodded before going to lie back down on the sofa.

After a few minutes, Jay walked into the living room with two bowls of soup on a plastic tray and two bottled waters.

"Do you really think Senator Bell is just going to take the jump drive and let us walk away?" I asked as I sat up and took the soup. "What if he takes it and we still end up charged with murder?"

Jay sat down next to me. "I don't know what other choice we have but to believe this will all work out."

"So you think we'll get out of this?" I asked, skepticism filling my voice.

"I know we will."

I sipped my soup, then said, "This is some heavy stuff, Jay."

Jay looked like he was pondering the fact that we could be in real danger. "We just have to tell the senator we didn't look at the jump drive. We can tell him that Vonda left a note not to view the drive, or something like that."

"Yeah, right, like he's gonna believe that."

He sighed like he knew that wasn't a good idea. "Well, I just know that we have to let him know that if anything happens to us, the information will be made public. We'll tell him we kept a copy as an insurance policy and if we're harmed, he's going to go down."

I continued eating my soup, savoring the hot liquid as it flowed down my throat. I finished off the bowl, then placed it on the coffee table. "I can't wait for our lives to return to normal," I said, leaning back on the sofa.

Jay set his soup bowl down as well, then scooted over and pulled me close. "Me either, baby."

For the first time in weeks, I didn't want to pull away from his embrace. In fact, I sank into his arms. We stayed that way, dozing off, until Jay's phone rang. I pulled away, shaking off the sense of safety I felt in his arms. No sense in getting caught up in the mood, I reminded myself.

"It's Quincy," Jay said, looking at the caller ID.

He pressed the speaker button to answer. "Hey, Quincy. Please tell me you got the senator," he said, not wasting any time with small talk.

"Hello, Jay, and yes, God is definitely working in your favor," Quincy said.

I sat bolt upright. "He'll see us?"

"Yeah, I didn't think he would, but his assistant called me back in less than thirty minutes once I was finally able to track down my friend. That's unheard of, so whatever you guys have must be major." Quincy paused. "What *do* you guys have, Jay?"

"I'll explain everything to you later, but it's best that you don't know now. When can we go see him?"

I could tell by the hesitation in Quincy's voice he didn't like being out of the loop.

"He's at home in New Orleans right now, but he'll be back in the morning, so they said you can come at one tomorrow afternoon."

"Great."

"Fine," Quincy huffed, "but I really want to know what's going on."

"We'll tell you as soon as we can."

Quincy was obviously agitated, but he said, "Okay. But until then, you guys be careful, all right?"

"We'll be careful. Talk to you later."

Jay hung up the phone and I released a sigh of relief. Was this ordeal almost over? The fact that the senator had agreed to see us meant we were on the right track. That thug Max had said that if we got the jump drive, all our problems would go away. I sure hoped so. I didn't see the senator admitting to any wrongdoing, but he was at least going to hear us out. Now we just had to find a way to convince him that it would be in his best interest to make sure we stayed alive.

twenty-five

Everything about Bradley Bell screamed power. From his navy Armani suit to his custom-designed shoes, Bradley Bell looked like a man who could make things happen. In fact, he'd been doing just that, representing his home district for almost twenty years. For a brief moment, I understood Vonda's attraction. If I hadn't been caught up in the middle of a life-or-death situation I might have given him a second glance.

But I *was* right in the middle of a life-or-death situation, and Bradley Bell might very well hold the key to setting me free from the nightmare that had become my life.

"How may I help you?" Bradley said, a wide campaign smile across his face.

Jay eyed the tall, muscular man standing next to the senator like a pit bull guarding its master. "We need to speak to you privately," he said, turning back to the senator as he discreetly brought out the manila folder containing the files we'd printed out the previous night.

Bradley waved in the man's direction. "Oh, Sammy is my right hand. You never know when you might need protection from people who want to do you harm. He stays."

The finality in his voice let everyone know the topic wasn't open for discussion. The campaign smile was also gone, and Mr. Bradley Bell was all business as he took a seat behind his desk. He nodded toward Sammy, who stepped toward us and said, "May I temporarily hold your cell phones? The senator likes to make sure all his conversations are confidential."

While Jay handed his phone over without flinching, I hesitated, not liking being ordered around when we were supposed to be the ones holding the cards. We needed to let Bradley Bell know we were the ones in charge. But the look on Jay's face let me know that was a fight we didn't want right now, so I handed Sammy the phone.

Bradley intertwined his fingers and drummed them on his desk. "So my assistant tells me you have some information that you think may be of concern to me."

"Oh, we don't think, we know," I said.

Jay shot me a *Let me handle this* look and I shrank back. The last thing I wanted was my hotheadedness messing anything up.

"You know Vonda Howard," Jay said, posing it more as a fact than as a question.

The senator's eyes went to the top of his head as if he were thinking. "I can't say that I recall that name," he finally said. "As you can imagine, I meet a lot of people."

I didn't know what kind of game he was playing. If he didn't know Vonda, we wouldn't be here. Maybe he was trying to gauge how much we knew before he admitted to anything.

Jay dropped the manila folder down on the large mahogany desk. "Senator, I assume you are a very busy man, so let's not play games. Neither of us has the time."

That seemed to make the senator sit up and take notice.

"Okay, so if I do happen to know this Vonda, what does that have to do with anything?" Senator Bell asked.

"I think you know exactly what it has to do with it. Now, for the record, we had nothing to do with any illicit activities, blackmail, anything that Vonda may have been involved in. But since someone has involved us in it, we've discovered some things that might be unsettling," Jay said.

"What type of things?" The senator's aura of confidence was gone and trepidation covered his face.

Jay slid the folder across the desk. "Things that could topple some very powerful people."

Senator Bell eyed the folder hesitantly, then picked it up and opened it. We'd made a few copies of the land acquisition spread. The senator's reaction didn't change as he browsed the pages. Finally, he closed the folder and set it down on the desk. "And what would it take for those things to, uh, to disappear? How much money do *you* want?"

"We don't want any money. We don't want anything from you but for you to call off the goons," Jay said matter-of-factly. "Oh, and clear our names, since we all know we didn't have anything to do with Vonda's death."

"And leave us alone," I added. "Let us go back to our normal lives. We weren't involved in this and we don't want to be involved in this."

The senator rubbed his chin. "I don't know what you

think I have the power to do," he began, "or why you would even think I'd be involved in any illicit behavior, but let's say hypothetically, I were able to get these purported goons called off. How would a person be sure that you would keep up your end of the bargain?"

"My wife and I are very public people," Jay replied. "Even if we were to never go on radio again, people know us and we'd be hard-pressed to go into hiding. Neither of us has any desire to live our lives in fear that someone is out to get us."

I added, "We just want to be left alone. We don't care what you and Vonda—"

Bradley narrowed his eyes at me.

"Or Vonda and whomever she was involved with," I corrected. "We don't care what they were into. We just don't want any part of it. I don't know how you can do it, but I'm confident that you can assist us in letting the authorities know we had nothing to do with any of this."

He laughed as he turned to Sammy. "They give me too much credit."

Sammy chuckled on cue, then immediately turned serious again.

"I'm sure you know some people who know some people who can make all of this go away," Jay said. I was actually impressed with my husband's take-charge demeanor. Senator Bell was an imposing man, and he was known to strike fear in the hearts of most who came in contact with him. But Jay was holding his own.

The senator grinned, once again going into campaign mode.

"Again, I don't know what you think I can do, but I'd be willing to make some calls." He lost his smile. "However, I'm sure you watch enough television to understand why I can't simply take your word that that's all you want. How can I be assured there aren't any copies of this document you claim to have?"

Jay leaned forward, his knuckles resting on the senator's desk. "And I'm sure you watch enough television to know that we won't take your word either. There are only two copies. The master copy, which we will gladly give to you to make this nightmare go away, and an 'insurance copy,' tucked safely away, only to be released in the event that either my wife or I meet an untimely demise."

The senator nodded like he'd expected that.

"Look, Senator Bell," Jay continued, standing up in an effort to ease the tension, "I didn't even know I had the drive and neither my wife nor I even know what all this stuff on the drive means. We just know it was enough to get Vonda killed. Now, we're not saying you're behind that killing—we just don't want to be involved. As you know, we have very successful careers and don't want to get caught up in any scandal. We don't play these dangerous games. I messed up by bringing Vonda into our lives, but we just want to be left alone."

Senator Bell looked like he was deep in thought as he leaned back in his chair. Finally, he said, "Well, I'll say it again: I'm not quite sure I can help you, but I'll definitely see what else I can do."

He nodded toward Sammy, who stepped toward us and gave us our phones back. "The senator will be in touch if he can assist you in your dilemma," Sammy said as he gestured toward the door. "I'll see you two out."

We stood. Jay grabbed the folder and the senator reached for it. "No, sir. This isn't yours until you get back to me." They both held on to the folder, the senator glaring at Jay. "My wife is standing by the door and she will scream."

The senator gave a sly smile as he released the folder. "We'll be in touch."

"I hope so," Jay said.

The two of us slowly walked toward the door. I was literally shaking as thoughts of being shot in the back of the head as I walked away filled my mind. I shook the image away. We were in the middle of a congressional office. How much could really happen here?

"So how soon before someone gets in touch with us and lets us know if, um, the senator can help?" Jay asked once we reached the door.

"Go to the Four Seasons downtown. There will be a reservation for you under the name Samuel Hidenberg. Get a room and wait for our call." Sammy didn't say another word as he closed the senator's door.

"Hidenberg?" Jay asked, his shoulders finally sinking in relief.

"Yes, Mr. Hidenberg," I said. "It's the Four Seasons—who cares what name they call you? As long as it has a bed, I'm good."

twenty-six

'd never thought I'd see the day when I was in a plush hotel room with my husband with a picturesque view overlooking downtown D.C.—and he would be sleeping on the sofa.

When we'd checked into the Four Seasons, I had almost asked for separate rooms. But fear of Bradley Bell and his henchmen coming to murder me in my sleep had kept me from saying anything that might attract more attention to us. Jay did have the wherewithal to ask them to move us to a different room than the one we'd been assigned just in case they were up to some funny stuff. Though since we didn't have to show any ID as Mr. and Mrs. Hidenberg, I was sure Senator Bell could get to us no matter what room we were in.

I had offered Jay the bed, but he'd opted for the sofa, saying he wanted me to get some rest.

We both were obviously worn out after all we'd been through, so it hadn't been hard for either of us to quickly fall asleep.

Now, as I watched Jay as he slept, a sadness crept over me and I wished that I could turn back the hands of time. Maybe I should've been more patient. Maybe I shouldn't have been so bitter. How did I expect to change the rules of the game, then simply expect my husband to play along? Yes, if I could turn back time, I'd do a lot of things differently.

Jay finally stirred; then his eyes fluttered open.

"Hey," he said, when he noticed me staring.

I grabbed the hotel menu to try to look busy. The last thing I wanted was Jay knowing I'd been sitting up pining over him.

"Hey," I replied. "How did you rest?"

"Like a newborn." He stretched and sat up. "I guess I really needed that sleep."

I held up the menu. "Do you want me to order some breakfast?"

"We've barely eaten anything since that soup the other night, so yes, I'm starving," he said, rising and heading toward the restroom. "Order the lox, two waffles, and double bacon and sausage for me, please," he said before closing the bathroom door.

I flipped open the hotel menu and scanned the breakfast choices. By the time I called room service and placed an order, Jay was walking back into the bedroom.

"I've been thinking about all of this stuff with the senator," I told him after I hung up the phone. "I want us to be cleared, but at the same time, I don't want him to get away with what he's planning to do in New Orleans."

"I don't either, but we can't get caught up, Shannon," Jay warned. "We already know these people don't play, and if we try to double-cross him, I think Senator Bell wouldn't hesitate to have us killed in the blink of an eye."

"Oh, I'm not even thinking about double-crossing the man. But maybe Nicole could do something. You know she sometimes produces special projects for MSNBC. I'm sure they'd be interested in this."

"I think we already got her curious when we called asking questions. You know she's not going to be able to just let it die. She's probably already digging for information." Jay sat back down on the sofa and immediately began folding up the blanket he'd used the previous night.

"Yeah, but you know there's only so much she can find. And I understand not messing around with the senator, but maybe if Nicole makes some calls to the White House press office, or the Army Corps of Engineers, it will put the whole levee system under scrutiny. So maybe just her digging around will be enough to scare the senator off."

Jay shrugged, still not convinced. "I guess. I don't want to get involved, but you're right—if something happened to those people in the Ninth Ward, I'd never forgive myself."

"Okay, I'm going to send Nicole a text and tell her not to do anything until we talk to her," I said, picking up my phone. "This has to be handled delicately."

After I finished texting Nicole, I leaned back against the headboard. An awkward silence filled the room as Jay sat on the sofa and I moved to sit on the edge of the bed.

"So what do we do now?" I finally asked.

"I guess we wait until someone from the senator's office gets in touch with us." He picked up the remote to turn on the television. He began flipping through channels, stopping on ESPN and becoming immediately engrossed. I watched him watch TV for a minute until a knock at the hotel door startled us both. We exchanged worried glances as Jay slowly rose and tiptoed toward the door.

"Who is it?" he called out.

"Room service, with your breakfast."

Jay looked through the peephole; then his body relaxed. "Thanks, I'm famished," he said, opening the door.

"You're welcome. I think you'll enjoy our chef's specialties this morning," the waiter said as he wheeled the tray inside. He removed lids, poured coffee, then had Jay sign the receipt.

"Thank you," the waiter said, dropping the receipt on the tray. His smile faded. "Now, I believe you have something else I need to get from you. Do you have the jump drive and the folder of the stuff you printed out?"

As soon as he said that, I froze. Jay instinctively stepped over and in front of me to protect me. How had we not seen this predictable, waiter-who-was-really-a-killer move?

"If anything happens to us . . ." I began.

The man waved his hand, stopping me. "Nothing's going to happen to you. I guess," he added with a slight chuckle as he eased open his white jacket to reveal the chrome pistol in his waistband.

"We're not going to just give you the jump drive," Jay said.

"Not until our names are cleared. If you shoot us, everything on that drive will be on the morning news."

Jay was bluffing but I immediately thought that was an insurance plan that we needed to enact as soon as possible.

The man started toward us and I jumped as Jay balled up his fists and prepared to fight.

"Calm down," the man said, leaning over on the table and picking up the remote. He changed the channel to the local news station, then glanced at his watch.

"What are you doing?" Jay asked.

"Tried to time this perfectly," the man muttered, more to himself. He looked irritated but nodded as a breaking-news banner came on the TV screen.

"This just in," the morning anchor said hurriedly. "The manhunt for celebrity relationship couple Jay and Shannon Lovejoy is officially off." A photo of the two of us at a UNCF gala last year flashed on the screen. "Police in the Virgin Islands were preparing to issue a warrant for the couple's arrest in connection with the murder of D.C. resident Vonda Howard. This morning, we've learned that Howard's death has been ruled a suicide and all charges against the Lovejoys have been dropped. The couple has been missing since Howard's body was discovered at their sold-out relationship retreat a few days ago—"

The man flicked the TV off before the report concluded. Jay and I stood staring at the screen in disbelief.

"We're cleared?" I asked, stunned. Just like that, we'd been exonerated?

"Yes." The man held out his hand. "We've kept our end of the bargain—now I need that jump drive."

"You got it," Jay said, walking over to his jacket and retrieving the jump drive from the inner pocket. He took the drive and handed it to the man, then opened a drawer, pulled out the manila folder, and handed that to him as well.

"I don't need to check this to make sure it's legit, do I?" the man asked, waving the jump drive.

"No, trust me, we want this nightmare to be over," Jay replied.

"So these are the only copies?"

"These and the one that's locked away in case something happens to us," Jay said matter-of-factly. The insurance copy was actually floating in the cloud. I'd taken photos and uploaded them because we hadn't had time to print out a second set and copy the files to another drive.

"As long as we're clear, nothing will happen to anyone." The man dropped the jump drive in his pocket, tucked the folder in the back of his pants, under his white jacket, then turned and left the room.

We didn't move for minutes after he left.

Finally, I spoke. "Is it really over?" I whispered.

Jay turned and stared at me. "It looks that way."

"Thank you, Jesus." I sank into my husband's arms and cried tears of relief.

twenty-seven

Home had never felt so good. I walked across the living room, running my hand over the sofa, gently touching the lamp, relishing the sanctity and safety of my abode.

"Everything looks intact," Jay said, coming in from the kitchen. He'd wanted me to wait in the car while he checked out the house just to make sure everything was fine. But I'd been so anxious to get inside that I'd followed him anyway.

Jay grabbed the remote and flipped our big-screen TV on. It was almost noon and he wanted to see what the news was reporting on us.

We both stood and watched as the noon newscasters recapped all that had happened. I was so grateful to be done with this mess that I didn't even care that the anchor was talking about Jay's "alleged affair with the deceased."

"You know there's no way Vonda killed herself," I said when the news story went off.

"We both know that, but I guess when you're powerful like the senator, you can get a death report to say whatever you need it to say," Jay replied. "All I know is, I don't care about the details and I don't care to know the details. The bottom line is a suicide means we're off the hook."

Bradley was definitely a powerful man. Just that fast, he'd been able to make this go away. No, he was definitely not someone I ever wanted to cross, but I knew my business with Bradley Bell wasn't quite over yet.

"I can't believe we were able to get him to cooperate just like that," I said.

"Yeah, but we know he was desperate to keep that information from coming out."

"Do you think he'll still move forward with his plans now that he knows people know?"

Jay shook his head. "I'm not sure. But men like that think they're unstoppable. So he may just be arrogant enough to move forward like nothing ever happened."

I didn't know how I would stop it, but I knew I couldn't let that happen.

Jay let out a long sigh, then glanced around the room, like he, too, was relishing being there. He'd been staying at a friend's condo and I could tell by his expression that he missed our home.

Finally, he said, "Well, I guess I'll go start getting some more of my stuff together. I know you wanted me gone as soon as we got back."

I hesitated as I stared at him, a mixture of emotions running through me. "You don't have to go right now. It's been a long few days. You can get your stuff tomorrow. And honestly, I . . . I don't want to be here alone just yet."

His eyes roamed up and down my body and his face bore an expression that almost looked like one of love. I shook that thought off. If anything, that was nothing but lust. After all, we'd been through a lot. "Nah, as much as I would love to stay, it's probably best."

I nodded, pained by his words. As Jay headed upstairs, I made my way into the kitchen to pour a glass of pinot grigio. Yes, it was still early, but after the week I'd had, I felt like I deserved a glass of my favorite wine, no matter the time.

Holding my wineglass, I made my way back into the living room, once again savoring my surroundings. I wondered if this place would feel the same when Jay left for good. My thoughts were interrupted by the ringing cell phone.

"Hello," I said, answering it.

"Shannon!" Nicole exclaimed. "Girl, I saw the news. You just don't know how happy I am."

"Not half as happy as me." I sighed.

We made some more small talk, and of course Nicole pushed for details on the New Orleans situation. But the last thing I felt like doing was rehashing everything right now.

"Okay, I'm going to give you some time to pull yourself together," Nicole said, giving in after begging for details for a fifth time. "Besides, I was calling because Riley wants to see you and Jay pronto."

Riley was the radio station manager and he was the most

anal-retentive man we knew. He was probably reeling that Jay and I hadn't bothered to make contact with him over the past few days. It was bad enough Jay and I had been off the air for over a month. I knew Riley was furious about everything.

"Dang, we've barely had time to process anything," I said. "Can he give us time to recover?"

"He's heading out of town in the morning, so he said it was imperative that you guys come in and see him or you, and I quote, 'may find yourselves without a job.'"

I rolled my eyes. That was an empty threat. With all the money we made for that station, Jay and I weren't going anywhere unless we wanted to go. Unfortunately, little did Riley know, but our show might very well be on its way to ending permanently. Still, I decided we did owe him a conversation.

"All right. I'll get Jay and we'll be there shortly." I gulped down the rest of my wine, then went upstairs to get my husband.

twenty-eight

Jay had not been thrilled about the idea of us going to see our boss. He kept fussing about how we needed time to recuperate from our ordeal, but I'd managed to convince him that we needed to go in and update Riley on everything that had happened.

Now I wasn't so sure that had been a good idea. We'd just finished running down the nightmare that had been our life for the past week and all Riley was worried about was us getting a divorce.

"Yeah, yeah, yeah, I'm glad you're safe," he said once Jay had finished explaining how we'd gotten away. "But please tell me the rumors that I'm hearing about you two getting a divorce aren't true," he said.

Riley was the consummate radio man: overweight, disheveled, and with graying hair that was thinning on top. He sat behind his desk, looking at us like we were crazy.

"Riley—"

"And when were you going to talk to me about it?"

"We just now started moving in that direction," Jay said.

"Moving in what direction? That's not an option," Riley said matter-of-factly. "The Lovejoys are a team. I'm selling the *couple*. I'm not selling Jay Lovejoy. I'm not selling Dr. Shannon Lovejoy. I'm selling the Lovejoys, with an *s*, the couple." He was flustered, like the idea of us separating would be devastating to him personally.

I cut my eyes at him, waiting to see if he was serious. He was.

"Well, we're sorry to burst your bubble, Riley, but we aren't for sale," I said.

"Yeah, Riley, it is what it is," Jay added.

"No, it is what you make it," he corrected. "And I need you guys to make this work."

"If only it were that easy." I sighed. The wave of his hand dismissed that thought.

"You're a therapist. I know you have some therapist friends you can go talk to. What's the problem? It can't be money, because you're rolling in that." Riley shrugged like he was really bewildered. "Infidelity? Everybody cheats. Man wasn't meant to be monogamous. If Jay screwed around with this Vonda woman, God rest her soul, go get you some on the side and call it a day."

That comment made Jay grimace, but Riley didn't notice, as he continued.

"If it's failure to communicate? Go away for the weekend and talk the whole time. Whatever it is, work it out." He sat forward in his seat like he'd solved all our issues.

"Riley, we appreciate your concern," Jay said, shaking his head, "but we're doing what's best for us."

"Are you miserable?" he asked Jay bluntly.

Jay looked down. "No, but—"

"Are *you* miserable?" he said, turning to me.

"No," I said.

"Is he beating you?"

"Of course not," I said.

Riley threw up his hands in exasperation. "Then what's the problem? And don't give me that irreconcilable differences baloney. That's a cop-out for people who think it's easier to give up than fight for their marriage." He took a deep breath, then turned around a five-by-seven picture of him and his wife, Sarah, that sat on his desk.

"Do you see that?" he asked.

"Yes, Riley, we know you and Sarah have been married for thirty years," I said, wondering what his point was.

"Do you think it's been all peaches and cream? No," he answered for us. "Sometimes I watch her sleeping and wish that she would just stop breathing in her sleep. Hell, half the time I don't even like her, but at the end of the day, I love her, and I know there's nothing better out there for me. My wife is good to me. She's good *for* me. There's no obstacle we can't overcome. That's what marriage is all about. Now, I know you think I'm just worried about my moneymakers, and honestly . . . I am. But I'm shooting to you straight: work it out. You two are good together. You belong together. I know you've been through a lot. We've been running repeats for several weeks and having guest hosts, but people want the real deal. So take a little more time off, pull yourselves together, and I'll see you two the day after tomorrow."

I couldn't help but laugh for the first time in days. "Wow, we were kidnapped, fugitives on the run, wanted for murder, and we get a whole day off. Thanks."

"Don't mention it. I'm a generous man," Riley replied, ignoring my sarcasm.

He stood and headed toward the door, where he paused, looking back at us.

"Just go home, have some hot, steamy sex, talk about your problems, and work it out." He turned and walked out the door, his words drifting in the air.

twenty-nine

While Riley's words had touched me, they obviously hadn't done a thing for Jay, because on the ride home, he'd told me that since he was so tired, he'd wait and leave in the morning. His not leaving at all had never even come up, and I'd found myself wishing morning would never come.

It had been a night of tossing and turning. I had lain awake for most of the night, watching the red digital numbers inch closer to 8 a.m. I knew that was the time Jay usually woke up. And this morning would be the last time he woke up in our home.

The thought tied my stomach in knots.

I was so full of regrets. Granted, I'd never be able to reconcile Jay cheating on me, but just like he'd driven me to cheat with Ivan, had I driven him to do the same with Vonda?

And did it even matter now?

I pulled myself out of bed, catching sight of my reflection in the full-length mirror. My hand immediately went to my stomach. I hadn't wanted to wait a few more years for a child. That had been the whole reason for my change in attitude. Now, who knew how long I'd have to wait. And unless I was willing to have a baby out of wedlock, my biological clock would be all ticked out by the time I found another man, fell in love, and got married.

I shook off that thought. I wasn't trying to marry another man. I wanted the man I was already married to. That hard reality slapped me fully awake.

"Then tell him that," I mumbled to myself.

"Are you in here talking to yourself?" Jay said, startling me.

I glanced up at my husband. He was wearing his running gear. I frowned. He only ran when he was stressed, when he needed to clear his head. We were out of the woods. So what was he so stressed about now?

"You went running?" I asked.

He shrugged. "Yeah, you know I'm dealing with a lot and, um, just needed some fresh air. Figured I would go for a run, then, ah, you know, come back, and, um, get my stuff together."

We stood in awkward silence for a minute; then Jay said, "Well, I'm going to go ahead and get to moving my stuff. I need to go grab the suitcases."

I didn't reply as our eyes met.

"Umm." Jay shifted uncomfortably. "I shouldn't be too long." He turned to leave and my heart began to race.

"Jay," I said, stopping him.

He slowly turned to face me. "Yeah?"

Just tell him, tell him you want to try to make it work! "I, ummm, I . . . do you need any help?" I asked.

He looked at me like he'd been hoping I was about to say something different. "No. I'm good. I think I can manage."

"Okay" was all I replied.

He looked like he wanted to say something more, but turned and walked out the door instead.

I went into my closet to throw on my running clothes. I needed to get out of there, go clear *my* head. The way I was feeling right now, I'd have an emotional breakdown watching him pack his stuff, then walk away from the home, the life, that we had built.

I took off running down the street and around the corner. I inhaled the brisk D.C. air as my feet connected with the pavement. I had just passed the neighborhood newsstand when a newspaper caught my eye. I stopped in horror as I read the headline. "Senator Bradley Bell Bombshell!"

An angry-looking picture of Senator Bradley Bell was front and center. It had obviously been taken as he walked into his congressional office. I read a few lines of the story, quickly paid for the paper, then raced back home. I must've made record time as I went barreling through the front door.

"Jayyy!" I screamed.

Jay came racing downstairs, his eyes wide like he was bracing for the worst. "What is it?"

"Look at this," I said, thrusting the paper toward him.

Jay looked at the newspaper. "What is this?"

"What does it look like? It's an article on the senator," I said, my voice laced with panic. "He's being questioned on the land deals in New Orleans."

Jay quickly scanned the story. "How did the newspaper get this information? Do you think Nicole said anything?"

"We haven't given Nicole any details. Besides, she wouldn't do anything without talking to me first. And she dang sure wouldn't give this information to the newspaper. She'd be doing a special report herself."

Jay shook his head in stunned disbelief. "Then where did they get the story?"

"I have no idea," I said, my heart racing. "It didn't come from us, but I guarantee you, Senator Bell is going to think it did. This man is dangerous. This puts us right back in danger." I actually found myself shaking in fear. "I thought this nightmare was over."

Jay continued reading the article, his mouth open in shock. "We didn't have anything to do with this."

"You know that and I know that, but he's not going to believe it," I cried.

Jay stomped over to the bar and snatched up his cell phone off the counter. "Well, we just need to tell him we didn't have anything to do with it. I don't want him sending any of his goons over here to mess with us." Jay spoke into the phone, "Siri, call Senator Bradley Bell's office." After a brief pause, the phone connected and Jay said, "Yes, I need to speak with the senator. . . . I understand that, but can you please patch me through to his cell or something? Tell him it's Jay Lovejoy. He'll want to take my call."

I watched my husband pace back and forth across the living room as he waited. Finally, he said, "Senator Bell, thank God you took my call. Look, I'm sure you've seen . . . No, I just wanted to call and assure you that neither my wife nor I had anything to do with that information being leaked. . . . Maybe Vonda told someone else." Jay stopped talking and pulled the phone away from his ear. "He hung up."

Fear filled me. Were we being thrust back in the middle of this mess? Were we going to have to go on the run again? No way could I continue to live like that. "We have to convince him that we had nothing to do with this."

"He was livid. He's not trying to hear anything we have to say." Jay picked up the paper again. It was a short article, without many details, but it definitely contained enough to cause trouble for the senator. "This says the newspaper received an anonymous call that the senator was involved in some shady land deals in New Orleans. But they keep saying it's unconfirmed."

"Well, why would they report it if it's unconfirmed?"

"Because the *D.C. Dispatch* is a tabloid paper whose publishers don't care about the facts. They report rumors all the time."

"But now that the story is out there, the legitimate press is going to jump all over it." I shook my head as the severity of the article sank in.

"Exactly, and that's probably what whoever gave the *Dispatch* that tip wanted."

"The question again: who would do that?"

"I have no idea, but I think I know who does."

We looked at each other as if we were thinking the same thing.

"Keri," we said in unison.

"I told you there was something shifty about her," I said. "I bet she did this."

Jay grabbed his keys. "Come on. Let's go talk to her and find out what the hell is going on."

It took less than twenty minutes before we were back in front of Keri's apartment. But as we pulled up, I saw a carpet-cleaning truck backed up to the stairwell. Hoses were running into the apartment and the door was wide open.

Jay knocked on the door, but the man cleaning the carpet obviously couldn't hear over the whir of the steamer, so Jay eased into the room and tapped him on the shoulder.

The man jumped, then removed his headphones and cut off the machine.

"Sorry, dude, I was in a world of my own," he said.

We looked around the empty apartment.

"We're looking for Keri, the woman who lives here."

The man shrugged. "Obviously, she doesn't live here anymore."

"Do you know where she went?"

He put his headphones back on. "Nope. I just got the order to come and clean the carpet. You might want to check at the front office." He turned the steam cleaner back on and resumed cleaning.

"This is definitely not a good sign," I mumbled, as we turned and headed to the building's leasing office.

Jay led the way into the small office. "Excuse me, we're looking for Keri, from apartment 1112," he said to the man sitting behind a big desk looking frazzled as he reviewed some papers.

"Yeah, you and everybody else," the man said without looking up.

"Do you have any idea where she is?" Jay asked.

The man released an irritated sigh and looked up at us. "If I did, I'd have my money. She just bailed. And she owes me two months' rent. Just left in the middle of the night. So if you find her, do me a favor and let me know. She left the apartment in shambles." He went back to sifting through his papers.

It was obvious the leasing agent couldn't help us, so we thanked him, then made our way back to the SUV. Inside, we sat contemplating our next move.

"Let me try to call Keri again," Jay said, tapping the screen of his cell phone. "Her number's still here from the other day," he said when he caught me side-eyeing him.

I threw my hands up. "I didn't say a word."

Jay groaned and hung the phone up. "The number's disconnected." He paused. "What if something happened to her too?"

"Nothing happened to her or she wouldn't have packed," I responded. "She took off, that's what happened to her."

Jay looked like he was really thinking. "Why would she leave in such a hurry?"

"Keri is on the run." That's the only answer that made sense.

"On the run from what, though?" Jay asked.

"Probably because she's in a whole lot deeper than she's letting on, and now she's spooked and decided to take off."

"How are we going to find her? She could be anywhere, and I feel like she's the only hope we have of getting answers," Jay moaned.

I sat deep in thought, racking my brain. Something was on the edge of my mind, something that I felt could lead us to Keri.

"She didn't go too far," I said, as it dawned on me what that something was.

"How do you know?"

"Remember the letter I was reading when we were there? From the nursing home about her grandmother?"

"So? Maybe she doesn't have a relationship with her grandmother."

"No, there was a picture on Keri's mantel of her and this old lady holding a birthday cake next to the woman's bed. I bet that's her grandmother. Maybe she knows how we can find Keri."

"So you think her grandmother is in a nursing home?"

I tried to recall the name I had seen on the notice. "Westhaven," I said, snapping my fingers as the name came to me. "Her grandmother is in Westhaven Nursing Home. That's the name that came up on the phone's caller ID and that was printed on that past-due bill. And her name is Eloise Walker. I think that we should go pay Ms. Walker a visit; maybe she knows how to get in touch with Keri."

"It's worth a shot," Jay said, shrugging.

"And at this point," I said, "it's all we have."

I didn't know what we were going to do if we found Keri, but I knew we had to do something—even if that meant dragging Keri to the senator's office ourselves so she could tell him what she knew. The bottom line was, I refused to spend my life worried about Senator Bradley Bell and his thugs, and if Keri was the only way to clear this up, we couldn't rest until we found her.

Jay was just about to back out of the parking lot when he turned to me.

"What?" I said, confused as to why he was staring at me.

"We make a pretty good team," he said with a smile.

My first instinct was to respond with sarcasm, but instead, I returned his smile. "We do, don't we?"

thirty

had never been on the inside of a nursing home—my grandparents were all dead by the time I was a teenager, and my parents hadn't lived past sixty—but it smelled just as I'd imagined it would: like mothballs and old people.

Thank goodness for the sweetness of the colorful bouquet Jay had thought to stop and pick up on our way there. The flowers made us look like official visitors as we made our way into the building.

We approached a robust woman with graying hair sitting at the information desk. She wore a name tag that read BERNICE.

"Good afternoon, we're here to see Eloise Walker," Jay said.

The woman looked up over her cat-eyed glasses.

"Haven't seen you here before," she said.

"I'm her nephew from Mississippi," Jay said with a big, cheesy grin. "My cousin Keri is going to meet us here later."

"Okay," the woman said, turning her attention back to her *National Enquirer* magazine. "Mrs. Walker is in room 12A. She might not recognize you. Half the time, she can't remember her own name."

I stared at him as we walked down the long hallway. "You're a great liar," I said, only half-kidding.

"Look, I'm just doing what I need to do to get us in here," Jay said, his tone defensive.

I let the issue drop and made a mental note to stop with the sarcasm. I didn't want to be the angry black woman, but what so many men failed to see was that they were the ones who made us angry. Pain has a way of sparking fury. Even so, we'd had some decent moments these past few days, and I didn't want to ruin them with an anger that wasn't good for anyone.

Jay eased open the door to Mrs. Walker's room. Inside, an elderly woman sat in a rocking chair, staring out the window. She turned toward us, long, stringy gray hair framing her face. She pushed some stray strands out of her eyes and squinted in our direction.

"Who is it?" she said.

I couldn't tell if the woman was half-blind or what, but she was definitely struggling to make out who had entered her room.

"I'm Sara, and this is Tony," I slowly began, shrugging at Jay as I approached her with measured steps. "We're friends of Keri from school." I almost said *college* but quickly changed my mind, since I wasn't sure if Keri had actually gone to college.

"Oh, you'll have to excuse me, baby, I can't remember much these days." Mrs. Walker laughed and turned back to the window.

"That's okay, I have a hard time remembering things my-self," I said, easing to her side. It dawned on me that Jay and I were so anxious to find Keri that we hadn't really talked this plan all the way through.

"What can I do for you?" Mrs. Walker said.

I looked at Jay. He shrugged again, so I just began spinning a story. "Well, today is Keri's birthday," I began, "so we wanted to—"

Mrs. Walker stopped rocking and frowned in confusion. "It's November? But I thought we just celebrated Palm Sunday."

I exchanged glances with Jay. "I told you, I have a hard time remembering things too. You are so right."

I knelt in front of the old woman. "I don't know if you know, but Keri has been quite depressed lately. And we're just trying to catch up with her so we can take her out and cheer her up or something."

Mrs. Walker shook her head like that couldn't be right. "But Keri said she's going away for a while."

"That's because she was so sad. You know what," I said, clapping my hands together as if a great idea had just hit me, "why don't we throw her a surprise party today?"

"Today?"

"Yes, you know how happy parties make Keri!" I hoped I wasn't totally off base.

The woman slowly nodded, as if she was trying to make herself remember.

I continued talking. "We could throw Keri a small birthday

party. Right here. Nurse Bernice already said it's okay. Tell you what, let's play a game. You call Keri and we'll make up a story to get her here; then when she gets here, we'll yell, 'Surprise!'"

Mrs. Walker continued shaking her head doubtfully. "I don't know about this. I watch my friends play bid whist at five o'clock, and I was just about to take my afternoon nap."

"It'll take Keri, what, an hour to get here?" I said. "That'll give us enough time for Tony here to run and get your granddaughter a cake and you can get a quick nap in."

She was quiet, as if she was contemplating it.

"Don't you want to make Keri happy?" I asked. I felt awful about using this poor old woman, but desperate times called for desperate actions.

"Yes, she's the only one who comes to see me," the woman said, her voice filled with sadness.

"Yes, exactly. She needs this. She was just telling me the other day how much stress she was under. And something like this would brighten her day. Don't you agree, Jay?"

"Tony," Jay corrected, shaking his head.

"That's what I said," I said, grimacing. "Let's go ahead and call Keri now. Do you know her cell phone number? I have it but it's in the car."

"Yes. I . . . I think she has a new phone. It's in my drawer, in my Bible."

I walked over, opened the drawer, and pulled out the Bible. I found the paper and dialed the number, making sure I committed it to memory. As soon as it started ringing, I handed the phone to Mrs. Walker.

"Tell her they're about to put you out of your room because your bill hasn't been paid," I whispered.

Mrs. Walker shook her head. "Oh, no, I don't like lying."

"Oh, we're not lying," I quickly retorted. "It's a surprise." Mrs. Walker took the phone, doubt still written all over her face.

"Keri, it's your grandmother," she began, her voice filled with hesitation.

I nodded, encouraging her with a smile.

"Um, baby, I need you to get down here right away. . . . Well, these people here, they say it's a problem with my room. Um . . ." She looked at me. "What did you say to tell her?"

I grimaced again. "Your bill hasn't been paid," I whispered.

Mrs. Walker nodded. "Oh yeah, they say the bill hasn't been paid and I have to go. Come down here, baby. Can you come now? I don't want to leave." She paused, then took the phone away from her ear. "She wants to speak to the nurse."

I looked at Jay and he motioned for me to take the phone.

I took it and began speaking in a nasally tone. "Hi, this is Sylvia," I said.

"Sylvia, who are you and where's my grandmother's regular nurse?" Keri demanded.

"Well, I'm the one who handles financial matters."

"I don't have any financial matters! What the hell is going on?"

"It appears your grandmother's bill hasn't been paid for two months, so we're preparing to move her out." I flashed a reassuring smile at Mrs. Walker, who seemed anxious at the idea of lying to her granddaughter.

"Are you crazy? I paid my bill two months ago."

"I'm sorry, but our records indicate otherwise."

"Well, your records are wrong!" Keri yelled.

"Well, if you claim you paid it, bring a copy of the cleared check down here on Monday and we'll get it all straightened out, but in the meantime, we're going to have to move your grandmother out because we have a waiting list for this room."

"Move her where?" I could feel Keri's anger through the phone.

"Well, unfortunately, we'll have to send her to a shelter for the elderly."

"Are you insane? You're not moving my grandmother! I paid the freakin' bill!"

"Well, is there any way you can come bring a copy of the cleared check to us now? Because of the high level of fraud, we're not allowed to accept faxes or emails as documentation."

"This is ridiculous," Keri huffed. "I can't come down there right now."

"Well, we're left with no choice but to move your grand-mother."

Keri uttered a string of curse words, before finally saying, "Ugggh, I'm on my way, and all I know is my grandmother better get a free month for all this hassle."

She slammed the phone down and I turned to Jay and smiled. "She's on her way."

"I don't like lying to my granddaughter." Mrs. Walker shook her head, clearly distressed.

I gently patted the old lady's arm. "Oh, but this little white lie will all be worth it," I said, leading her over to the bed. "For now, you just lie here and get some rest, and, Tony, you can run to the grocery store down the street and pick up a cake."

Jay shook his head as I walked him to the door.

"Do I really need to go get a cake?" he whispered.

"No, just wait outside a few minutes."

He nodded. "Okay." He stopped and looked at me. "Oh, and Shannon?"

"Yeah?"

"You're a pretty good liar yourself." He didn't smile as he walked away.

thirty-one

couldn't believe we were about to do this, but I knew we
hadn't been left with much choice. We needed answers, and
Keri was the only one who could give them to us.

"You really think this is going to work?" Jay whispered.

"It better, because it's our last hope," I replied.

He glanced down at the old woman, who had dozed off
and was peacefully sleeping. We'd been waiting for forty
minutes. Nurse Bernice had come in, and I'd assured her that
everything was fine and we were waiting on Keri, so the
woman had pretty much left us alone.

"I don't know. I feel bad about using the old woman," Jay
said.

"I do too. But you'd think you'd feel worse about looking
over your shoulder all your life," I replied.

"You have a point there."

We paced the small living quarters for about twenty more
minutes before the door to the room swung open.

"Grandma?" Keri called out as she barreled into the room. She had her hair pulled back into a ponytail and a tight jogging suit on.

As soon as she stepped in the room, I jumped up and slammed the door closed.

"What the—?"

Jay immediately covered Keri's mouth. Keri slapped his hand away.

"Shhh," he said, gently pushing her against the wall. "We don't want to hurt you."

"What the hell do you think you're doing?" she asked, trying to wiggle from his grasp. "Did you do anything to my grandmother?" Her eyes frantically looked over at her grandmother.

"Of course not," I replied. "She's sleeping."

Keri jerked free, then walked over to make sure that her grandmother was fine. Satisfied that she was, Keri spun toward us. "I'll ask you again: what are you doing here?"

"What does it look like?" I said, walking toward her.

"It looks like you broke into an old lady's room and are now trying to take me hostage."

Keri pushed her way around Jay and headed toward the door. "I'm going to call security."

"Do you really want anyone to know that you're here? I'm sure there are some people looking for you," Jay said, stopping her in her tracks. "I mean, if *we* could find you, it shouldn't be any problem for Senator Bell's people to find you too."

Keri spun around, her eyes wide with fear. "Why would they want to find me?"

"Obviously, you're the one behind the story in the newspaper," I said.

Her eyes darted from side to side. "Wh-where did you get that idea from?" she stammered.

Jay regarded her, his eyes narrowed. "The story ended up in the media anyway, and the way I see it, the only people who knew about the blackmail were me and Shannon and you and Vonda. Bradley Bell is pissed. He thinks we went back on our word. He thinks we double-crossed him."

"And we didn't," I said. "That means, if we didn't, and since Vonda's dead, you're the only person left on the list of suspects."

"Why am I being dragged into this? I didn't have anything to do with this." Her voice cracked; it was obvious that she was terrified.

"Because you're the only other person who knew about the senator," Jay said.

She glared at Jay a moment before saying, "What makes you think that?"

"Look, little girl," I said, slamming my palm up against the wall, causing Keri to let out a small scream, "we're not messing with you. Our lives are in danger because you want to play games."

"Get away from me!" Keri shouted. She moved away from the door, her chest heaving up and down as she glanced over to make sure the commotion hadn't awakened her grandmother. "I didn't have anything to do with anything," she protested.

"Whatever! You and your bimbo friend came up with this grand scheme to get rich off a shady politician and it's blowing up in your face."

"Stop talking about Vonda like that!" Keri yelled, before catching herself when her grandmother squirmed. She lowered her voice. "Women like you are so freakin' pathetic. You want to hate the other woman, when it's your husband you need to be hating," she spat. Her eyes were filled with venom. "Vonda didn't owe you a damn thing. *He* did." She jabbed a finger toward Jay.

I took a step back to calm myself. It wasn't that I was buying into Keri's speech; the way Vonda had tormented me in the Virgin Islands, I had a right to hate that tramp. But I knew we wouldn't get anywhere if I continued to badger Keri.

I made eye contact with Jay as if to tell him to step in and handle this.

"Look, Keri," he began, holding his hands up, "we're just trying to get to the bottom of what's going on. If you say you didn't have anything to do with the story in the *Dispatch*, then who else knew? Who would go to the press?"

She huffed, rolled her eyes, then folded her arms across her chest.

"Please, Keri. These are our lives here," Jay pleaded. "None of us are safe."

She blew out a frustrated breath. "Fine. The only other person who knew what Vonda was doing is Vincent."

"Who is Vincent?" Jay asked.

Keri smirked. "Vonda got around."

"What?" both Jay and I said in unison.

"I didn't stutter. Vincent is the true love of Vonda's life. They just have a volatile relationship, so they don't work well together. She thought you would help her finally get him out of her system, but they have history," Keri said.

Jay looked dumbfounded. I was mortified. First Bradley Bell, now this Vincent guy. So now there were more men in this DNA-swapping chain I'd unknowingly been involved in? I was getting mad all over again.

"H-how do you know she told him?" Jay stammered. He probably was thinking the same thing I was—exactly what kind of woman was Vonda Howard?

"Because Vincent had a way of creeping back into her life whenever he felt like it. And Vonda had some loose lips during pillow talk. She messed up and told him one night, and truth be told, I think he was the one egging her on to blackmail the senator."

"Why didn't you tell us this from the start?" I asked.

"Look, I told you I don't want to get involved. Senator Bell may be a legit thug, but Vincent is a real-life thug. I know for a fact he's killed someone once before. I'm not trying to become one of his victims," Keri said.

"Where can we find this Vincent?" I said.

Keri cut her eyes at me. "If I tell you, will you get out of here and leave me alone?"

"Yes," I said, as Jay nodded.

She sighed. "He's always hanging out at Carrington's Pool Hall over on 133rd. You'll know him because he's the undefeated pool champion there; his picture is hanging on the wall. Just do not tell him I told you where to find him. He can get crazy and I don't need the drama."

"Thank you, Keri. You're a lifesaver," Jay said.

She walked over to the door. "Whatever. Just get out of my grandmother's room and don't ever come back here." She moved over to the bed and gently brushed her grandmother's hair. Whatever scandalous things Keri had done, there was no denying her love for her grandmother.

"Go!" Keri snapped when we didn't move.

I headed toward the door. That was one request I would happily oblige.

thirty-two

It wasn't hard to spot Vincent Murray. If the photo below the "Pool Champion" title hadn't been enough, his loud, boisterous behavior would have been sure to draw everyone's attention his way.

"Vincent Murray?" Jay asked, tapping the man on the shoulder.

Vincent stopped in the middle of a hearty laugh and spun around on his barstool. There was nothing remotely attractive about this man. He had a rugged, unkempt look and his matted Afro looked like it hadn't been washed in weeks. The smile left his face as he looked Jay up and down. "Who wants to know?"

"Look, I'm not the police or anything," Jay said.

"I'll ask again, who wants to know?"

"Can we talk?" Jay looked around at all the people staring at him. "Privately?"

"Dude, I don't know you like that."

I stepped in. "I think you do."

One of the goons standing in the back of the pool hall spoke up. "Yo, my girl listens to y'all." He turned to Vincent. "This is that cat that was messing with Vonda. The radio dude."

Vincent's eyes lit up in recognition. "What happened to Vonda?" He directed his question to Jay. "She's a lot of things but she ain't suicidal, and word on the street is that she took her own life."

"She didn't kill herself," Jay said. "And I didn't kill her."

Vincent studied us for a minute, then said, "Follow me." He led us to the back of the pool hall. Four of the goons followed us.

Obviously, Vincent was over his grief, because he spun around and said, "If Vonda tried to play with the big dogs and got burned, that's not my problem."

Jay didn't address his comment. He got straight to the point. "Look, we know you are now the one behind the blackmailing of Senator Bell. And we believe that you sent the information to the newspaper."

Vincent turned his nose up. "You don't know a damn thing," he said casually.

Jay held his hand up in defense. "Honestly, we don't really care. We just don't want the senator thinking we're the ones behind it."

Vincent strode over to a chair and sat down. He leaned back, folded his arms behind his head, and said, "What does that have to do with me?"

"We were just hoping that you would, um, you know, go to the police with what you know."

Even as the words left Jay's mouth, I could tell we had a better chance of getting Donald Trump to apologize to Barack Obama for birtherism than we did of getting this man to help.

All five of the men burst into laughter. "You must be on drugs," Vincent said.

"At this point, the senator isn't going to believe anything we say, so maybe you can tell him we're not involved," Jay said. I was quivering next to him, too afraid to speak.

"And why, Mr. Superstar, would I do that?" Vincent asked, the laughter dying down.

"Look," Jay began.

"No, *you* look, playboy," Vincent said, his tone firm as he sat back up. "I don't know you from a hole in the wall, so I couldn't give a rat's ass about you. All I know is you were screwing my girl. But Vonda had a way of trying to piss me off, and since chicks come and go, I ain't sweating that. But you can rest easy—the senator knows who he's dealing with."

"So he knows it's you?" Jay asked. That possibility had never even crossed our minds.

"You said it yourself: this here is major." Vincent sighed. "Look, let me enlighten you. This ain't about you. This is between the big dogs now. That little nugget I dropped to the *D.C. Dispatch* has him ready to do whatever I say."

"So he knows you're behind the article?" I repeated, stunned that he was so forthcoming with information. But

Vincent seemed to be the bragging type, so I guess he was taking pleasure in revealing that he was calling the shots.

Vincent continued. "He knows I wasn't playing around, and he knows there's more where that came from." He stopped and exhaled like he was trying to decide how much to reveal. "And since he doesn't want my next package to be to the *New York Times*, he's ready to play ball."

I exhaled in relief. If Senator Bell knew Vincent was behind the article, did that mean we were out of danger?

"Come on, Vincent, you seem like a man who can't be conned," Jay said.

"Damn, skippy," Vincent replied. "I do the conning." He smiled, and I wondered what in the world my husband was doing. I wanted to grab Jay's hand and tell him, *Let's go and let the big dogs work this out.*

"Do you really think Senator Bradley Bell is the type of man who's going to let anyone blackmail him and get away with it?" Jay asked.

That must've hit a nerve with Vincent, because the smile left his face and Jay seized the moment.

"I mean, he's probably planning to meet up with you somewhere to pay you off, and before you can turn the corner good, he'll have someone put a bullet in your back."

Vincent shifted uneasily. "I know what I'm doing," he said, his voice losing some of its edge. "This ain't my first time at the rodeo."

"Yeah, but how many other powerful politicians have you blackmailed?" Jay said.

Vincent was cocky, but he was definitely small-time compared to a crooked United States senator. He had no idea the type of people he was dealing with.

"Even if you do know what you're doing," Jay added, "even if he lets you walk away today, he's not going to rest until he deals with you. People in power are like that."

"What's that supposed to mean?" Vincent asked, like we were really getting on his nerves.

Jay shrugged. "I'm just saying. . . ."

Vincent huffed like he'd had enough. "You know what? You," he said, looking at Jay, "and you," he said, pointing at me, "need to bounce before I show you how gangsta I can be."

I had an eerie feeling that Vincent Murray had just signed his death warrant and I wanted no part of it.

"You're absolutely right, Mr. Murray. You got this." I grabbed Jay's arm and pulled him toward the door. "We're bouncing."

thirty-three

couldn't believe we were back on the air with all the drama going on in our lives. I'd been adamant that we tell Riley we couldn't come back just yet, but Jay had convinced me that it was for the best that we remain in the public eye. Our names had been cleared, and now that the senator knew we weren't behind the article, I assumed we were out of danger.

Even though Jay had been planning to leave, after the visit with Vincent, he insisted on staying with me a couple of days, just to make sure. He was worried that the senator might get antsy and decide he needed to get rid of everyone who knew anything.

"We need to go back to work because the senator will be less likely to cause trouble if we stay in the public eye," Jay had told me last night.

So after the show today, we were doing an interview with a few local stations, then shooting interviews for CNN, MSNBC, and Fox.

While in no way did I like being in danger, I loved how protective Jay was being.

"Are you guys ready to do this?" Nicole said, gently patting my hand.

"Ready as we'll ever be," I mumbled. We'd agreed that we would just talk about our ordeal for a few minutes, then ease back into our normal routine.

I hadn't been able to get Vincent out of my mind. How did he really expect all of this to play out? Was he meeting with the senator now? He was a fool if he thought he could just blackmail the senator, then go about his business. I brushed away thoughts of Vincent Murray. He was making his bed, so whatever happened was his problem.

"Relax, babe," Jay said, reaching over and touching my arm. "Sorry," he said, pulling his hand away. "Habit."

I couldn't help but smile at the loving way he touched me. It made me nostalgic, but I quickly reminded myself not to read anything into it.

"We're going to be fine," he added.

The show's opening music began, and Nicole gave Jay the cue to start.

"Helloooo, lovely listeners, this is Jay and Dr. Shannon Lovejoy, back on the air and coming to you in real time," he began.

I took a deep breath and leaned into the microphone. "And we are so happy to be back with you, live. Thank you so much for bearing with us through our hiatus and as we ran our best-of-the-Lovejoys shows."

"And unless you've been under a rock"—Jay chuckled—"you know that our Lovejoy retreat turned into something out of the movies for us."

From there, Jay and I took turns recapping our ordeal. We did leave out the why behind our kidnapping, blaming it on the wrong place at the wrong time. Jay was careful and glossed over his relationship with Vonda, simply saying she had begun stalking him, and for that, I was appreciative. We had decided we wouldn't announce the divorce until later, and the last thing I wanted was sympathy calls from people.

After we finished our spiel, the phone lines lit up with people offering their best wishes and prayers, and even a few people digging for gossip. One caller even told us, "I know there's more to this story."

Jay laughed and politely told her, "We've shared what's important."

But it was the last caller who changed the entire upbeat mood.

"Hi, Jay and Dr. Shannon," the woman began. "I've been listening to your story, and like everyone else, I'm just so thankful that you guys made it through. You two saved my marriage with your advice and words of wisdom. I've been reading some of the stuff in the papers and I don't know what's true and what's not. I don't really care. I just wanted to tell you both that you have a gift and something like this can break even the strongest foundation. But the fact that you two made it through speaks volumes. I just want you to know I'm praying that this ordeal happened for a reason. I know that may sound crazy, but sometimes when things are broken, God has an uncanny way of fixing them."

Jay couldn't help but smile. "I think I've heard that before."

The woman chuckled. "You have. That's exactly what you told me when I called in a year ago."

I instantly remembered this caller. She had been a reprieve from our typically distressed callers. Her spirit had been so warm. Both she and her husband had called in together. She'd had an affair because she'd thought he was having one. She'd later found out that he wasn't, but by then it was too late—the damage had been done, and her husband had been devastated.

"Well, I'm glad my words could help you," Jay said.

"Oh, they did more than help," the woman replied. "We are now better off than we ever were because you and Dr. Shannon convinced us that our love was worth fighting for. That's a magical gift you have. And sometimes we're so busy using our gifts to help others, we don't use them for ourselves."

The studio was quiet as both Jay and I stared at each other. The woman must've known her words were impactful, because she said, "Just think about what I'm saying. Think about what *you* said to me: everything happens for a reason. I'm keeping you both in my prayers."

She didn't say another word and hung up. Jay and I remained silent until we heard Nicole yelling in our headsets, "Wrap! Wrap! We're going over!"

Jay jumped, apologized for the silence, then gave our standard goodbye. I jumped in on my cue, thanking the listeners for tuning in.

Once we were off the air, neither of us said a word as we gathered our things to leave.

thirty-four

This was the way things should be—me relaxing on the sofa with a novel, and Jay in the kitchen, whipping up his specialty, shrimp spaghetti, for lunch. I wished we could stay like this forever. The only thing that would make this scene complete would be a little Jay running around.

That thought made me lose my smile. That thought was the reason why this whole scene was simply a mirage, because it was just a matter of time before Jay would be gone for good, because my desire for a little Jay had destroyed my relationship with my big Jay.

We had gone to work in separate cars, so we'd left the radio station without saying anything about that last caller. Then, we were so busy with interviews all day, so by the time we got home, neither of us addressed it, instead falling into this natural rhythm.

I turned my attention back to my novel. It was a new one, called *Sister Surrogate*, about a woman who was desperate to have a child. I had been enjoying the book, but when I thought about my current situation, I decided now maybe wasn't the time to dive into that subject matter, so I moved it to my to-be-read file and stood to go see if Jay needed help.

The television was on mute when I noticed a picture of Senator Bell. I picked up the remote and turned the volume up.

I watched for a few seconds, then called for Jay.

"Jay, come here. Hurry!"

"What's wrong?" he said, racing into the living room.

"Look." I pointed to the TV. Once again, a breaking-news banner was flashing across the screen.

"This just in," the anchor began. "United States Senator Bradley Bell has been taken into custody in connection with the death of Vincent Murray, a local resident with an extensive criminal record who was found dead last night."

"Dead?" Jay said, his mouth dropping open. "Vincent is dead?"

"Shhhh," I said.

"Reporter Stephanie Jameson is in the field with the latest." The anchor tossed to a reporter in the field. "Stephanie, why would police think the senator is connected to the death of Murray? And does this have anything to do with the allegations that surfaced yesterday morning about the senator and land deals in New Orleans?"

"Rick, this story is unfolding by the minute," Stephanie began, her voice urgent, like she was on the cusp of a major story.

If only you knew, I thought.

"In fact, we are in front of the police department, where authorities are expected to bring the senator in any minute. Apparently, Murray was trying to blackmail the senator over those reported land deals in New Orleans. But just moments ago," the woman said, "we were handed this envelope." She held up a manila envelope. "Inside was a zip drive containing video of the entire transaction in which Murray allegedly met the senator to collect his blackmail money. A private investigator working a totally unrelated case for a woman trying to catch her cheating husband captured this video."

My mouth fell open as I watched Senator Bell and Sammy, his bodyguard, approach Vincent in the back of what looked like an apartment building. There was no sound, but the image was clear as day. Vincent stood face-to-face with the senator. Sammy walked over with a duffel bag, and handed it to Vincent, who opened it up and looked inside. The private investigator must have known something illicit was going on, because he zoomed in to get a shot of what appeared to be wads of money in the duffel bag. A huge smile crossed Vincent's face as he closed the bag, reached in his pocket, pulled out something, and handed it to the senator.

"I bet he's giving him a copy of the jump drive," I said. "And here we thought we had the only copies."

The video jumped to a gray Nissan Sentra and the reporter continued talking. "The private investigator followed Murray, who got into this car a few blocks over. That car was being driven by an unidentified woman."

Both Jay and I gasped as the video zoomed in to a side view of Keri.

"Police say another vehicle registered to the senator's office followed Murray back to his apartment. A few minutes later, a neighbor found Murray dead with a gunshot wound to the head."

"Where is the young lady who was driving the car?" the anchor asked.

Stephanie shrugged. "That's the million-dollar question, Rick. She has disappeared, along with the money. Police don't believe she's behind the shooting of Vincent Murray, because a witness saw her drop Murray off, then leave. But again, they are searching for the woman to question her about last night's events. They're asking anyone with any information to give them a call. In the meantime, police say they believe they are on the cusp of an even larger investigation. Of course we'll keep you updated." She tossed back to the anchors in the studio, who began banter about the story.

Jay picked up the remote and flipped the television off.

"I don't know what to be more shocked about, the fact that the senator has been arrested or the fact that Keri was working with Vincent all along," I said.

"Why would she even tell us about him, though?" Jay asked.

I shook my head. "I don't know. Maybe she planned to take all the money all along and she knew that if she led us to Vincent, we'd be able to confirm that he was the blackmailer and tell the police.

"And when the dust cleared, the police would think only Vincent and the senator were involved," I finished. "And though we could tell them about Keri, by that point she would be long gone with the money."

I had to hand it to the girl—I would've never given her credit for being so conniving.

"Well, if the senator is behind bars, at least this means we're safe. Even if he gets out, which I suspect he will, he knows we're not involved," Jay said.

"I'm not so sure," I said. The more I thought about this, the more I felt like this wouldn't truly be over until I knew if Keri had been behind everything the whole time.

"What do you mean?"

"I mean, there are still a lot of unanswered questions, like why would Keri sell out Vincent? Did she decide to just pick up where Vonda left off? And how do we know the senator doesn't still think we're working with Keri?"

Jay slapped his forehead. "Oh, good grief, I just want this to be over."

"Yeah, me too," I replied. "But it's not. And it won't be until we track Keri down and find out what kind of game she's playing."

"If the police can't find her, what makes you think we can?" Jay asked.

I smiled. "Well, Mr. Lovejoy, I think we've proven we're some superb sleuths."

Jay laughed. "You got that right. Who would've ever thought that?"

"The police don't even know who Keri is, so they wouldn't even know where to start looking for her."

He smiled. "And we do?"

I nodded. "Looks like we need to go pay another visit to our dear friend Mrs. Walker."

thirty-five

Why in the world couldn't we leave well enough alone? I asked myself that a million times as Jay and I drove to Westhaven Nursing Home. Maybe our nightmare was over. Maybe we didn't have anything to worry about.

But it was that *maybe* part that I couldn't live with.

I followed Jay inside the nursing home, hoping we'd have the same luck we'd had before. There was a different woman at the front desk.

"Hi, we're here to see our aunt, Mrs. Eloise Walker," Jay said.

The young, perky desk attendant frowned in confusion. "I think Mrs. Walker is gone already," she said.

"Gone where?"

"Her granddaughter is moving her out today." The woman scanned a log in front of her. "Oh, I'm sorry, she hasn't left yet, so she should still be in her room." The woman flashed a smile.

"Miss Patterson!"

We all turned to see the nurse we'd seen on our first visit, Bernice.

She came stomping toward us. "I realize you may be new," she told the woman at the desk, "but rule number one is that we don't give out private patient information."

The younger woman's eyes widened in fear. "Oh my God, I'm so sorry. They said they were family."

"Well, they lied." Bernice glared at us. "They were just here yesterday with that lie, and almost cost me my job." She moved to block our path. "Now, I have been given strict instructions that Mrs. Walker will not be having any visitors, especially you two. So I'd appreciate it if you would please leave. Otherwise, I will be forced to call security."

Jay held up his hands. "Hey, no need to call security. We're leaving."

"So much for that idea," he said, once we were back outside. We climbed into the SUV. I put my hand up to stop him from turning the ignition.

"What are you doing?" I asked.

"I'm leaving. You heard them tell us we couldn't see her."

"I also heard them say her granddaughter is coming to move her out today."

Jay smiled as he realized I was saying we should wait. "Where do you think Keri is taking her?"

"Well, she's rich now, so she's probably taking her across the country to some private facility."

"So we're just going to sit here and wait on her?"

I nodded.

"We could be waiting a long time," Jay warned.

"Then we might as well get comfortable," I said, shifting in my seat.

We sat in the vehicle and waited. Neither one of us wanted to chance dozing off and missing Keri, so we chatted about everything—general stuff at first, our own relationship. I was honest about my feelings regarding the vasectomy. He apologized and told me he was just scared. It was a deep, insightful conversation—one we probably should've had a long time ago. I realized that I wanted to keep digging in this story because I liked being close to Jay.

"I guess Riley was right. Maybe we just needed to sit somewhere and talk," Jay said.

I glanced at my watch. It hadn't felt like it, but it had been three whole hours since we first pulled up to the nursing home.

"Yeah, it's just a shame we couldn't make time to talk until it was a little too late," I finally said.

Jay nodded in agreement. "Yeah, but—"

"Hey, hey, look, it's Keri," I said, cutting him off as I hit his arm. I pointed toward the parking lot. Keri had just pulled into a space in the second row. Both Jay and I jumped out and raced over to stop her before she reached the door.

Keri froze at the sight of us. It looked like she was trying to decide if she was going to take off running. Instead, she said, "What do you two want? Why are you following me?"

"We need to talk to you," I said.

Keri glanced around nervously.

"Don't worry, we're by ourselves," Jay said.

"For now," I added, pulling out my cell phone.

"What are you doing? Are you calling the police?" Her voice was full of panic. "Why are you guys harassing me? What have I ever done to you?"

"Only lied from the first day I met you and got us caught up in all this drama," I snapped.

"I didn't get you caught up. Your husband would be the one who did that."

Checkmate, I thought. But now wasn't the time to go there. Instead I said, "What kind of game are you playing, Keri?"

"I'm not playing any kind of game."

I began punching numbers on my phone. "Either you be honest, or I'm dialing the last digit to the cops. They'll be here before you know it. You know everyone on the force is looking for you and we're the only ones who even know your identity."

Keri sighed in defeat. "What do you want to know?"

"We want to know what kind of game you have us caught up in," I repeated.

"I told you I'm not playing any game. You two are the ones who don't know how to leave well enough alone, and I definitely don't have you caught up in anything." She rolled her eyes and folded her arms.

"No, the senator probably thinks we're in on this with you guys," Jay said.

"What are you talking about?" Keri replied. "Bradley knows you're not involved."

Jay and I exchanged shocked glances. "Bradley? And how do you know that?" Jay asked.

"Because Vincent told him he was acting alone," she said, looking back and forth between the two of us. She nodded as if she'd figured out why we were so worried. "Oh, you thought he was still after you?"

"We weren't sure," Jay said.

"Well, rest easy," Keri said. "When big-mouth Vincent decided to pick up where Vonda left off, he made it clear that he was acting alone. He didn't even give me up. I think he wanted them to think he was intelligent enough to pull it off by himself. As if."

Jay narrowed his eyes, not missing what she was saying. "Give you up? Were you in with Vonda on this all along?"

Keri *tsk*ed but didn't reply.

"Were you?" Jay repeated. "Did you help Vonda pull this off?"

"Please," Keri snapped, like she was offended. "Vonda wasn't smart enough to pull this off either."

Jay frowned in confusion. "What does that mean? Vonda was the one sleeping with the senator."

"Nobody was sleeping with the senator," Keri said with an attitude.

"What?" Jay and I said together.

"But you said—" Jay began.

"I know what I said," she snapped. "But Vonda wasn't sleeping with him."

"Then how did she get the jump drive?" I asked.

Keri pursed her lips as she cocked her head. "Let's just say

Senator Bell underestimated the power of his lowly adminis-
trative assistant."

"Excuse me?" I said.

Keri huffed like we were working her nerves. "I worked in
his office while I was in college. Senator Bell decided that the
only way I could advance would be to have sex with him; then
he had the nerve to have me fired when I refused to do so. Not
only did he get me fired, but he got my scholarship revoked.
That scholarship was the only way I was able to stay in school.
So needless to say, with it and my job gone, I had to drop out.
I stumbled across his little land deal while working for him.
He, like every other man I know, underestimated my intelli-
gence. I held on to this information for six months, hoping I'd
never have to use it, but waiting on just the right time in case
I did. And the day I got fired was the right time."

I scratched my head. This didn't make sense. "So this was
about a vendetta?"

Keri's eyes were raging with fury. "It sure was. I worked
my ass off trying to get ahead and do things the right way
and the oh-so-powerful Senator Bradley Bell decided he was
going to ruin my life because I refused to have sex with him!"

"Wow," Jay said, as her revelation set in. "So how did
Vonda get involved?"

For a moment, I didn't think Keri was going to answer.

"Keri, please? If we wanted to cause any trouble for you,
the cops would be here, not us."

Keri took a deep breath and said, "I didn't want him to
know where the blackmail was coming from, so I had Vonda

contact him. I promised to give her some of the money if she helped me out. Only her dumb behind couldn't follow simple instructions and she told her stupid-ass ex-boyfriend."

"So *you* got your friend killed?" Jay said.

"I didn't kill her," Keri protested. She paused as a young couple passed us in the parking lot. When they were out of hearing distance, Keri turned back to us. "We knew the risk of what we were doing. I had a plan, but Vonda didn't stick to it. She's the one who used her home phone to call the senator's office to try and blackmail him, claiming she blocked her number before calling. How stupid is that? All it took was a call to the phone company, and they tracked her down. So *she* got herself killed, not me!"

"So it doesn't bother you at all that your best friend was murdered because of a plan you came up with?" I asked.

"Of course it does," Keri snapped, her eyes watering. "But what am I supposed to do about it? And then Vincent comes in and tries to pick up where Vonda left off. I didn't want to work with him. I can't stand him. But since Vonda told him everything, I didn't have a choice. And guess what? He didn't want to follow my plan either, and look what happened to him."

"So I guess you won," Jay said, shaking his head.

"I guess I did." She defiantly folded her arms across her chest. She was trying to play hard, but I could tell she was scared to death.

"Now what?" Keri finally said. "You got the whole story. Will you please leave me and my grandmother alone?"

We stared. I was torn. I didn't condone blackmail, but if what Keri was saying was true, the senator had basically ruined her life. Then there was the fact that by even bringing this issue to light, Keri had potentially stopped what could've been a catastrophic disaster in New Orleans.

After all this attention, even if the senator beat the murder charge, no way would he do anything with the land in New Orleans. So maybe Keri deserved to be paid, even if it was with ill-gotten money.

"You know what?" I finally said, looking at Jay. "Our name is cleared, and Senator Bell knows we're not involved, which means he should leave us alone. So as far as I'm concerned"—I looked back at Keri—"we're not in it."

Shock covered Keri's face. "Are you serious?"

Jay nodded in agreement. "Hey, it's like my wife said, we're clear, and personally, I'm tired of playing detective, so I think we should let the cops do their own job."

"So you're not gonna turn me in?"

I shook my head. "Nope. Think about it, you might've saved thousands of people in New Orleans. Because if Senator Bell really had planned to cause another disaster, a lot of people could've lost their lives."

Keri bit her bottom lip like she was thinking. "Wow, I never looked at it like that."

"Yeah," I continued, "because you took the jump drive, people know about what the senator was planning. So the way I see it, you're entitled to the money, and as far as I'm concerned, we're done. We can't say that the police won't stop searching for you. And Senator Bell may not have put two and two together and figured out your connection, but he's a smart man. It may be just a matter of time."

"I'll be long gone by the time he figures it out."

"Good luck to you and your grandmother. I think it's admirable that you didn't take off and leave her," Jay said.

Keri looked wide-eyed. "That wasn't even an option. That's my grandmother. She raised me."

I couldn't help but smile at Keri. That girl was going to be all right. She had a survival instinct that was going to let her take care of herself—and her grandmother.

"Well, if you'll excuse me, I need to go get my grandmother out of here. The security here sucks." Keri flashed a grin. She headed toward the door, but then stopped and turned to face us. "And thank you so much for not turning me in."

"Thank you for finally giving us some closure," I said, looking at Jay. Our nightmare was officially over. Now it was time to work on closure for our marriage.

thirty-six

Things were supposed to have returned to normal. And they had. Jay was in one room and I was in another. Gone was the fear of thugs, con men, and crooked senators. It had been replaced with the emptiness that had consumed us before Vonda came crashing into our world.

Keri was probably long gone by now, with the senator's money. As I'd expected, Senator Bell had been released from jail this morning, and had held a press conference "vowing to fight the unjust charges" against him. I had debated calling in an anonymous tip, but then decided I didn't have to. Every media outlet in the country was all over this story, including MSNBC, for whom Nicole was working on a special investigation. It was just a matter of time before someone dug up the dirt on their own.

"Hey, I got the last of my things loaded into the car. I just have a few more things. I'm pretty tired. If you don't mind, I'll just get them tomorrow."

I nodded. I'd been upstairs, aimlessly watching rap videos on MTV. I hated rap, but I needed anything to drown out my reality—the reality that my husband was actually packing up and leaving.

Jay stood in front of me, his blue-and-white Nike warm-up suit dotted with specks of dirt from him moving boxes all day.

I was heartbroken. After that caller had encouraged us, and we'd really talked, I'd thought that things had gotten better.

But then, we had said very little yesterday after returning from the nursing home. The quiet tension that resided in our home took over the minute we stepped back inside. The only conversation we'd had had been over breakfast, when Jay questioned whether we should talk about any of this Bradley Bell stuff. I didn't really want to. We'd agreed to tell our listeners that we were going our separate ways, so with that hanging over me, I really had no desire to talk about anything else. I couldn't help but think about my mother's curse about karma. Maybe this was my payback for not being a good wife—losing the man I really did love.

We were really about to go our separate ways for good.

"Before I go, I need to say once again how sorry I am—about everything," Jay began.

My first thought was to deliver a sarcastic response, but I no longer had the energy. So I simply said, "Me too."

I wanted to grab him and beg him to figure out a way to work it out. But I felt frozen. This time, it wasn't even about pride. I just couldn't bring myself to beg him to stay.

"I guess we can sit down and talk about assets later?" he said.

"Can we just have the attorneys do that?" The anger and bitterness were gone. Right now, only pain filled my space. And every minute that Jay stood in front of me, the pain deepened.

"That's cool." He stood awkwardly in the bedroom doorway. "Oh, in case I didn't tell you, you're a good private eye."

That brought a smile to my face. "You told me we were good together."

"We were," he replied.

"This all was kind of fun. We did have a little adventure, huh?" I said, managing a small laugh.

"Yeah. It wasn't fun at the time, but it was exciting now looking back." He paused. "I just wish we'd done more of those types of things over the past year."

"What, run from police, thugs, and crooked politicians?"

He chuckled. "Not that part. The adventure part."

"Yeah, hindsight is a powerful thing," I said solemnly.

Jay nodded as the awkward silence settled between the two of us again. Finally, he said, "Okay, I guess I'll see you later at the station."

I briefly looked away and simply shook my head. He waited, like he wanted to say something else; then he turned and left the room. When I heard the door chime signaling his departure, I pulled my pillow close to me, my hand gently caressing his side of the bed. I closed my eyes and tried to inhale his scent. I wanted to capture it before I could no longer remember it. Emptiness filled my heart—an emptiness I wondered if I'd feel for the rest of my life.

thirty-seven

Today was the day of reckoning. We were officially about to let our listeners know about the divorce and my heart had never felt heavier.

"Are you sure this is the way you want to handle this?" Nicole said as I handed her the scripts for the show.

I nodded. "We owe it to our listeners. And besides, it's just a matter of time before the public finds out, so we'd rather do it this way ourselves. Go out on top."

"Well, Jay's already in there," Nicole said. "He's been at his desk for two hours, not saying a word, just sitting there like he's lost in thought. And he barely spoke when he walked into the studio."

He probably wants to make sure he doesn't come out looking like the bad guy, I thought. Well, he didn't have to worry about that. I was tired of being bitter and angry. I was going to do this show, make our announcement, and then go on my merry way.

We still hadn't figured out what we were going to do about the show long-term. Personally, I wanted to let Jay have the show; I had no desire to continue dispensing relationship advice. But I didn't know if that was possible, since Riley had made it clear he wanted the team. Riley had been so angry when we'd announced today would be our last broadcast. Of course, he'd tried to talk to us some more, but he'd given up in disgust, saying only that he thought we "were making a grave mistake."

He was in a meeting with the bigwigs right now to figure out their next move. I imagined that included suing us for breach of contract. I couldn't focus on that, though. After the ordeal I'd been through, I just wanted to move on.

I walked into the studio, sat in my regular spot, put my headphones on, and got settled. My eyes met Jay's and had he not been clear regarding his wishes, I would've definitely thought this was something he didn't want to do.

But this was something we both wanted. I'd wanted it first, then he'd accepted it.

Thankfully, the show was about to start, so we jumped right in. There was a flurry of callers who wanted to continue to comment on everything we'd been through; then there were a few who wanted the typical advice. The hour went by in a blur and I couldn't really recall all that I'd said. I only knew we were nearing the end of the show because Jay said, "Well, before we wrap up, we have some news to share with our listeners." He briefly hesitated, then went on. "Today is bittersweet." He looked at me to allow me to take over. I didn't say anything. I was afraid that if I opened my mouth, I'd break out in tears.

Pull yourself together, I told myself.

"We've been bringing you love advice—on our own at first, me through songs, Dr. Shannon through her practice—and then together as the Lovejoy team for the past two years," Jay continued, when it became obvious I wasn't going to say anything. "It's a job that we both took seriously, one we were committed to giving our all to. We've loved helping heal relationships, helping couples rediscover the true meaning of love, and providing the glue to hold so many marriages together—"

"Unfortunately," I interjected, finally finding my voice, "we couldn't hold our own relationship together." My voice quivered as I spoke. "Some of you may have heard the rumors about my husband and me, and, well, it is with a heavy heart," I said, taking a deep breath and struggling not cry, "that we share with you—"

"That even the strongest of couples," Jay said quickly, cutting me off, "falter." He stared at me intensely, his eyes welling with tears as he continued talking into the mic. "We want you to know that we realize firsthand that marriage is something worth fighting for, and when you have that one person who God has designed especially for you, you don't give up just because things get hard."

Confusion blanketed my face.

"I . . ." Jay said, not taking his gaze off me. "We had come here today to tell our listeners that we had agreed to go our separate ways, and while it's been something I told you that I was okay with, the thought of one more day of waking up without you by my side has caused me unimaginable pain."

"Jay, what are you saying?" I forgot all about the microphone.

"I'm saying I love you. I love you in the depths of my soul," he said, his voice now quivering. "My love for you is captured in every beautiful memory of our past, detailed in vivid visions of our dreams and future plans, but most of all it's right now, in the moment where everything I've ever wanted in my life is sitting right in front of me. I know I've made mistakes, but if you give me the chance, I will spend the rest of my life making up for that. If you want kids, I'll give you a house full of kids. If you want us to walk away from all things Lovejoy, I'll do that. Just please don't leave me, Shannon."

Tears started streaming down my cheeks. I felt like my mind was playing tricks on me.

"One of our callers told us everything happens for a reason," Jay continued. "I believe that from the bottom of my heart. Everything we've been through these past few weeks has been so that I could appreciate the woman I married, and remember the reason God brought us together. I just realized my greatest joy comes when I'm making your heart smile. I can't lose you, baby."

"I don't want to lose you either," I cried as I removed my headphones and bolted from my seat and into my husband's arms as he stood.

It wasn't until we saw half the radio station standing in

the control room, clapping and crying, that I even remembered we were still on the air.

I pointed to the mic. "Jay . . ."

"Oh, man," he said, jumping back into his seat. "Sorry about that, everyone, but my wife and I got caught up for a minute." He looked at me and smiled. "That's all our time for now."

I slid back into my seat, leaned into the microphone, sniffling and wiping my tears. "Thank you for joining us . . . and make sure you live, laugh, and love." I turned to face my husband as our theme music filled the studio. "Because that's exactly what I plan to do," I said, as Jay rose, took me into his arms, and squeezed me like he never wanted to let go.

We were interrupted by a tap on the glass from the control room.

"Hey, guys," Nicole said. "I hate to interrupt this beautiful moment, but there's one more caller insisting on talking to you."

"We're off the air," Jay said.

"I know, but he's insisting and said that you'll want to talk to him."

Jay and I exchanged confused glances as Jay eased over to patch the call through.

"Hello," I said.

"Hi, sweetheart. It's Ivan calling about my money. . . . I hope you didn't think I forgot. . . ."

acknowledgments

Should I really do this again?

That's the question I ask myself every time I sit down to write an acknowledgments. I mean, some may wonder, when you've written as many books as I have, who else is there left to thank? What else is there left to say? Well, when you've been as blessed as I have been, how can I *not* thank those who helped me churn out another story? And, as a writer, I always have something to say.

First, let me tell you how this story came to be. It's a little different from what I usually write, but that's intentional. Several years ago, I sat down and started writing romantic suspense, because I love reading suspense books. But while I tried to steer the characters in one direction, they were stubborn and wanted to go in their own direction. So that's what they did, taking on a life of their own.

I had fun with this book, weaving Jay and Shannon in and out of situations. And along the way, I fell in love with them and found myself rooting for them to make it. (Here's where my sister would jump in and say, "You know these people aren't real." Lol.) But I lived with them and wanted the best for them. As a reader, whether you wanted them together or apart, I hope you were entertained by their story as well.

Now, for the thank-yous . . .

I'll keep this one a little tighter—simply saying thank you once again to my family: my amazing children, my loving mother, and my wonderful sister, Tanisha Tate. A special thank-you to my muse, Jeffrey Caradine, who pushes me, no matter what.

For the past decade, my business/writing partner, Victoria Christopher Murray, has continually helped me up my game. Thank you, sis.

My forever friends: Jaimi Canady, Raquelle Lewis, Kim Wright, and Clemelia Humphrey Richardson. You're the light in my hectic life.

As usual, thanks to my agent, Sara Camilli, and my editors, Lauren Spiegel and Rebecca Strobel. Thank you for all your hard work!

I could go on for days thanking all the book clubs, libraries, and readers who have supported my work. Please know that just because I didn't name you (this time), I still value and appreciate your support.

And, finally, thanks to YOU . . . my beloved reader. If it's your first time picking up one of my books, I truly hope you enjoyed it. If you're coming back, words cannot even begin to express how eternally grateful I am for your support. From the bottom of my heart, thank you!